SIAN BESSEY

KIDS ON A
MISSION

Uprising in SAMOA

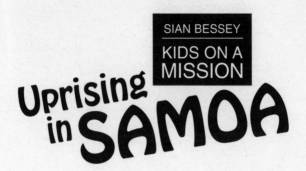

SIAN BESSEY

KIDS ON A
MISSION

Uprising
in SAMOA

a novel by

SIAN BESSEY

Covenant Communications, Inc.

Cover illustration *Uprising* © Rocky Davies; Cover background image by C Squared
Studios © PhotoDisc Green/Getty Images, Inc. Cover design by Jessica A. Warner,
copyrighted 2005 by Covenant Communications, Inc.

Published by Covenant Communications, Inc.
American Fork, Utah

Printed in Canada
First Printing: June 2005

11 10 09 08 07 06 05   10 9 8 7 6 5 4 3 2 1

ISBN 1-59156-890-0

For Anna—
who is beautiful inside and out

Chapter 1

"How much longer?" Emily yelled.

She shuddered as two blasting honks were followed by a short, sharp squeal. Covering her ears with her hands, she moved closer to her brother's bedroom door and shouted to Matt again.

"Matt! When are you going to be done?"

There was a moment of blissful silence. Then the door swung open to reveal Matt with a shiny, gold saxophone hanging around his neck.

"Finally!" moaned Emily, lowering her hands from her ears. "It sounds like you're strangling geese in there."

Matt grinned. "Hey, I must be getting better! Last time you said it sounded like a bunch of tugboats."

Emily rolled her eyes. "I don't know why you couldn't have chosen something a little quieter, like a kazoo or a triangle."

"Nothing's as cool as the saxophone," Matt said. He raised the mouthpiece to his lips and blew one long, low note just to prove it.

Emily sighed. "Well, how much longer do you have to practice? Mom's run over to Sister Nelson's to take her some tomatoes from the garden. She said she'll take us swimming as soon as you've finished."

Matt's eyes lit up. Swimming did sound a whole lot more fun than practicing the saxophone.

"I've already got my swim trunks on," he said. "It'll only take me a minute to put away the sax."

"Well hurry. I want to be ready when Mom gets back."

Already wearing her swimsuit, a pair of bright blue shorts, and her flip-flops, Emily followed Matt into his bedroom. She pulled her long, dark hair up into a ponytail while he carefully cleaned out his instrument.

"That's gross," she said, as the cleaning cloth came out of the saxophone damp with saliva.

"You should see the trumpets," Matt told her. "They collect so much slobber they've got a spit valve to empty it all out."

Emily pulled a face and turned her back on Matt and his instrument cleaning. She walked over to the bedroom window and looked out. There wasn't a cloud in the bright blue sky. Heat reflecting off the cement patio in the backyard shimmered through the air. On the other side of the backyard wall, Emily could see small clusters of missionaries walking between buildings at the Missionary Training Center. Their white shirts gleamed in the sunlight. She saw a couple of elders run their fingers around their collars, loosening their ties a little in the summer heat.

Watching the missionaries always reminded Emily of the short mission she and Matt had shared. Automatically, her eyes strayed to the old wooden shed that stood on the MTC grounds, right beside their own backyard wall. The children had discovered their own special mission call in that shed. They'd been drawn there by a strange light glowing around the wooden door—the same light that had been glowing around the mission call envelope once they'd stepped inside. She and Matt had checked the shed many times since then, but they'd never seen the glowing light again.

Until now.

Emily's heart started pounding. She leaned forward, pressing her face against the glass of Matt's bedroom window. She was up high enough to see the shed clearly, but the sun was so bright and the reflection so strong . . . was she imagining things? Was there a bluish-white light shining through the crack around the shed door?

"Matt," she said urgently. "Come here."

Matt was kneeling on the floor. "What is it?" he asked, clicking closed the latches on the saxophone case.

"The shed . . ." Emily said. "I think it's . . ."

She didn't need to finish her sentence. Matt was immediately on his feet and beside her at the window.

"Can you tell?" Emily asked, not taking her eyes off the old wooden door.

Matt raised his hands to his eyes to shield them from the sun's glare. "Not for sure," he said slowly, an excited smile spreading across his face, "but I know how to find out. Come on!"

Chapter 2

Matt grabbed the flip-flops lying beside his bed and shot out of the bedroom with Emily close behind.

"Wait, Matt!" Emily called. "I saw it first!"

Matt slowed down long enough to open the back door. Then he was off again, running across the backyard to the large, old ash tree that hung over the wall. He stuffed his flip-flops into the back pockets of his swim trunks and began climbing the tree. Emily followed him up. Branch by branch, they wove their way up the trunk until they reached the thick, long limb that stretched out over the wall. Matt scooted along the branch to make room for Emily. Once they'd both straddled it safely, they stopped to catch their breath.

The thick canopy of leaves above their heads shaded them from the direct sun, but they had a perfect view of the old wooden shed. And from this vantage point, there could be no doubt. A strange bluish light was streaming out through the crack around the door.

Matt looked over his shoulder at Emily, his eyes alight with excitement.

"It's all happening again," Emily whispered.

"Yeah. Let's go check it out."

"But Matt." Emily reached out to grab her brother's shoulder. "If we go back to Germany, the Gestapo could be waiting for us."

Matt paused, reliving the last, tense minutes of their mission to Germany. Then he shook his head.

"No," he said. "We've talked about this a hundred times since we got back. If we end up going anywhere again, it'll be because we're needed. We're not going someplace just to get in trouble."

Emily wasn't convinced. "You don't need the Gestapo," she said. "You find trouble anywhere."

Matt grinned. "Well, let's go see where it is this time." And without waiting for a reply, he began crawling along the branch toward the wall.

Emily watched him for a few seconds, then groaned. There was no way she was going to let him go alone. Besides, her own curiosity and excitement were building. Maybe they really could help someone again. She waited until Matt leaped from the branch onto the wall, then she squirmed her way down the swaying limb and jumped onto the wall behind him.

They crawled along the wall until they were right above the shed. Then, on the count of three, they dropped onto the roof. The clatter of their feet hitting the tiles echoed across the MTC grounds, but as far they could tell, no one had heard. So, after waiting a few moments, the children slithered down the roof and jumped onto the soft grass below.

They ran around to the front of the shed. The eerie light was still streaming out around the door. Matt took hold of the doorknob.

"Ready?" he asked.

Emily nodded. Her mouth was dry, and she wasn't sure that she could speak even if she tried. Matt took a deep breath, turned the doorknob, and pushed. The door swung open to reveal the shed just as they remembered it—a small, musty room containing old gardening tools and a battered wooden desk. And on the desk was a long, white envelope, glowing brightly.

The children stepped inside. Emily closed the door behind them and watched as Matt picked up the envelope. She moved closer as he pulled out the piece of paper inside and unfolded it. Two black plastic name tags slid into his hand. Matt turned them over, and they both read the imprinted words. One said, "Brother Williams," and the other said, "Sister Williams."

Matt looked over at Emily, his eyes sparkling. "Look familiar?"

Emily didn't answer. She reached out to grab the letter, but Matt moved his hand just in time.

"What does it say?" she cried.

Quickly, he unfolded the piece of paper. Emily moved to stand beside her brother and they read the letter together. It was dated May 15, 1921, and written to Brother Matthew and Sister Emily Williams. The signature at the bottom was Heber J. Grant's.

"President Heber J. Grant again," Emily breathed in wonder. "But the date's different. It's even earlier than last time. He must've been the prophet for ages."

"Twenty-six and a half years," Matt said.

Even though she knew of Matt's love for numbers and dates, Emily looked at him with astonishment.

"I looked it up after we got home from Germany," he added with a shrug.

"Is it Germany again?" She anxiously looked back at the paper in Matt's hands.

"No," Matt said, pointing at a specific line. "Look."

Emily read the words out loud. "You are called to serve in the Samoan Mission of The Church of Jesus Christ of Latter-day Saints."

"Wow," Matt said. "Where's Samoa?"

Emily thought for a minute. "I think it's an island in the Pacific Ocean."

"Like Hawaii?" Matt asked.

"Yeah. But even farther away than Hawaii."

"Sweet!" Matt picked up his missionary name tag.

"Stop!" Emily reached out to prevent him from pinning on the name tag. "What're you doing? We don't know anything about Samoa or what we might find there."

"Sure we do," Matt disagreed. "It's just like when we went to Germany.

13

We know the most important thing—that we're needed."

Emily chewed her bottom lip, as she always did when she was nervous.

"Come on, Em," Matt encouraged her. "We'll be okay. Hey, maybe we'll even see the ocean!"

Emily took a deep breath and picked up her name tag. "All right. But how about we say a prayer before we leave the shed this time."

Matt smiled happily. "That's what the best missionaries would do," he said.

With trembling fingers, Emily pinned her name tag to her swimsuit. She looked up in time to see Matt finish attaching his name tag to his red T-shirt before the bright light in the shed began swirling around and around. A low-pitched humming filled the small room. Then—just as suddenly—it stopped.

Emily and Matt looked at each other and then at the shed door.

"You say the prayer," Emily whispered.

Matt bowed his head and, in a quiet voice, prayed for guidance and protection. Then, pausing just a moment after the "amen," he stepped forward and grasped the doorknob. Carefully and quietly, he opened the door.

Chapter 3

A wave of hot, damp air flooded the small shed. It was like opening the door to a steamy bathroom.

"Wow!" Matt breathed.

Emily didn't say anything. She just stood beside her brother, gazing around in wonder. They were standing on a balcony, overlooking a small clearing. A brilliant blue sky—bluer than the brightest blue crayon in a crayon box—looked down upon them. In the distance, as far as the eye could see, towering mountains reached for the sky. The mountains were completely tree covered and looked as though they were draped in dark green carpet. A misty cloud hung over the highest peaks, hiding the mountaintops and giving them an aura of mystery.

Immediately in front of them was a wide, grassy clearing. Tall palm trees grew around the area, their large leaves making soft swooshing sounds as they swayed gently in the breeze. Shorter trees grew in clumps between the towering palms, and even more shrubbery grew in a tangled mass of leaves and dazzling blossoms beneath them. Dirt paths criss-crossed the clearing, leading in and out of the trees.

The balcony on which they stood ran along the front of a fairly large, whitewashed, wooden building. Several doors opened up onto the balcony, and, at its far end, a set of stairs led down to the ground below. They could hear muffled voices coming from somewhere within the building, but there were no real clues as to what the building was used for.

"I wonder where we are," Emily said.

Matt shrugged his shoulders. "Somewhere in Samoa, I guess."

Emily frowned. "I know that! But what's this building?"

She leaned over the balcony, trying to get a better view of what lay beneath. A sudden movement at the edge of the clearing caught her eye.

"Matt!" She reached for her brother's arm and pulled him down into a crouching position beside her. "Keep your head low, but check out the palm trees over there." She pointed to her right.

Very carefully, the children rose just enough to peek over the balcony railing. A tall, dark-haired man was running toward the building from the direction of the palm trees. His only clothing was a dark blue cloth wrapped around his waist. His golden-brown skin was covered—head to toe—with swirls of black and red paint. In his hands he carried a long-handled knife with a broad blade and a vicious-looking hook.

The children watched until the man disappeared from sight, presumably to enter the building beneath them. Gingerly they inched upward again and peered down on the clearing.

"Look!" Matt gasped, poking Emily with his elbow and pointing toward the palm trees again.

Half a dozen men were stepping out from between the trees. Dressed just like the first man, each one carried a large knife or club. In single file, they ran across the clearing in silence, following the path the other man had taken. Then, they, too, disappeared into the building.

"Let's get out of here," Matt said. "Come on! Before anyone else comes."

Emily nodded. Slipping off her flip-flops, she hurried after Matt as he headed for the stairs in a crouching run.

It was hard to be quiet. The wooden balcony creaked with every footstep, and the stairs were even worse.

A man's voice shouted something from inside the building. Matt and Emily froze. Had they been heard? A chorus of male voices echoed the first man's words.

"Quick! While they're making enough noise to cover us," Matt urged.

He ran down the remaining stairs and raced around the corner of the building, with Emily right behind him. They didn't look back.

Matt spotted a narrow dirt footpath in between the towering trees. He headed straight for it and didn't stop running until his breath was coming out in short gasps and sweat was dripping from his forehead.

"It's so hot," he panted, leaning his head against a tree trunk.

Emily staggered toward him. "I think I'm going to melt!"

Leaves rustled above their heads.

"Aaaaah!" Emily screamed as a huge green ball dropped out of the air and landed with a thump at her feet. Seconds later three more rained down upon the children.

"Watch out!" Matt cried, jumping to one side just in time to miss being hit on the head.

Emily screamed again and ran for cover.

All at once the jungle was alive with noises. The leaves above shook, voices called out, and the sound of running feet and cracking branches echoed all around them. Matt moved to stand next to Emily, his head darting in every direction, trying to figure out where the sounds were coming from.

Suddenly a man burst through the bushes to their left. "Fiti?" he called. "Fiti, what's going on?"

"Up here, Misi Tomas," a voice called back.

Matt and Emily looked over at the tallest palm tree to see a pair of long brown legs appear beneath the lowest leaves. They watched in amazement as a boy climbed down the trunk of the tree—hand over hand, foot over foot— just like a monkey. Within seconds, he'd landed on the ground beside them, and after giving them a curious glance, he turned to face the man.

"I was just cutting down the coconuts," he explained. "I did not know that anyone was beneath the tree."

Matt and Emily stared at the large green balls on the ground. They didn't look anything like coconuts. They were at least double the size, and they weren't even brown and furry. The man, however, seemed to believe the boy. He turned to look at the children.

"I'm sorry," he said. "Are either of you hurt?"

Both children shook their heads.

"We're okay," Matt said. "We just didn't expect to be attacked by giant green basketballs."

The man's mouth twitched. "That is one of the hazards of walking through a coconut plantation," he said.

"This is a coconut plantation?" Emily asked in amazement. She gazed around at the tangle of trees and plants.

"It's badly overgrown," the man admitted, "but we're working on that."

"But those don't even look like coconuts," Matt said, pointing to the large green balls.

The man drew a long hooked knife out from under his belt and whacked the closest ball. With a crack, it split in two. Nestled in the center was a small, brown, furry coconut.

"Cool!" Matt said. He stepped closer for a better look.

"You've not seen coconuts before?" the man asked. "You must be new to the islands."

"We just got here," Matt said.

The man raised his eyebrows. "You speak the Samoan language well for newcomers."

Matt and Emily exchanged a quick look. They couldn't explain it. The gift of speaking a foreign language seemed to come with their mission calls.

"Uh, thanks," Emily said.

She shifted her feet uncomfortably. Then, before he could ask any more questions, she quickly added, "We're looking for the Mormon missionaries."

The man looked surprised. "Really? Well, you've just found one." He reached out and shook Emily's hand. "I'm Misi Tomas, one of the elders assigned to work at the mission school in Mapusaga."

"Misi Tomas?" Emily repeated.

"'Misi' means missionary," Misi Tomas explained. "Some of our English words are hard for the Samoans to pronounce. They call us all Misi and usually give us new Samoan names or change our names a bit. My last name is actually Thompson—but Tomas is easier. My companion, Misi Sami, is Elder Samuelson."

"And you're serving at a mission school?" Matt asked. "I thought you said this was a coconut plantation."

The missionary smiled. "Well, both are right. The Church runs one of the finest schools on the islands here in Mapusaga. Our schoolhouse is just over there." Although he pointed to his right, it was impossible for the children to see anything through the thick leaves. "This coconut plantation is also Church property, but it's been neglected for many years. The students are working hard to clear the land and make it more profitable for the village."

Matt and Emily looked around and, to their surprise, discovered that sometime during their conversation with Misi Tomas, a dozen or more boys had slipped out from between the trees and were standing just a few feet away. They seemed to range in age from about eight to eighteen, and every one of them had the jet black hair, deep brown eyes, and honey-brown skin of a native islander. They were wearing simple T-shirts along with white cloths wrapped and tied around their waists. The cloths looked like a cross between knee-length, baggy shorts and a skirt. Their feet were bare and dust covered. Several of them carried long knives, and they were all staring at Matt and Emily with a mixture of curiosity and wariness.

"Uh, I'm Matt Williams," Matt said nervously. "And this is my sister, Emily. We've been sent here as missionaries."

Misi Tomas raised his eyebrows. "It takes a while for messages from the president to reach us. I'm sorry. I wasn't expecting you. Did someone from the mission home bring you out here?"

"No. We . . . uh . . . we . . ." Emily looked at Matt helplessly. What could she say? *She* didn't even understand how it happened. "We just sort of arrived by ourselves."

Misi Tomas studied the children. His eyes moved from their flip-flops to their brightly colored clothes.

"Where are you from?" he asked.

"Utah."

"Provo."

Matt and Emily spoke at once, and a flicker of excitement crossed Misi Tomas's face. "I'm from that area. My family farms one of the largest orchards in Orem. I'll bet you've seen it."

The children looked at each other. They couldn't remember any big orchards in Orem—only homes, stores, and businesses.

"I don't think the orchard's there anymore," Matt ventured.

"It can't possibly be gone," Misi Tomas said. "I've only been out here ten months. And besides, I just heard from my brother, and he said they're expecting a good peach harvest this year."

Emily gave Matt a look of warning. "Matt doesn't mean that the orchard's not there *now,*" she said. "He just meant that . . ."

"It's not going to be there in the future," Matt finished for her.

Fiti took two big steps back and started muttering something under his breath.

"Enough, Fiti!" Misi Tomas said. "You know better than to believe in old superstitions."

The muttering stopped, but Fiti did not move closer.

"We really are here to help you." Emily prayed Misi Tomas would believe them. "We received a mission call from President Grant. He wouldn't have sent us to Samoa without good reason."

But Misi Tomas was no longer paying attention. He was staring at the path Matt and Emily had taken. His head was tilted slightly as though he were listening to something. Seconds later, the children heard it too—the sound of someone, or something, moving quickly through the bushes. All eyes were on the path when a young boy burst into the small clearing. He'd been running hard and was gasping for air. He staggered to a stop right in front of Misi Tomas and immediately bent over, leaning his hands on his knees as he fought for breath.

"Tama? What is it?" Misi Tomas put his arm out to steady the boy.

"You must come!" the boy said. "Come quickly, Misi Tomas. The council is meeting. Warriors are arriving in the village. The high chieftain, Magale, is talking of war."

"War? What do you mean?"

"The governor has offended Magale. Magale says that he will show the governor that the Samoan people's wishes are not to be ignored."

Misi Tomas's face turned pale. "Tama, are you sure of this?"

Tama nodded.

"We saw the warriors too," Emily said.

"Where? Where were they?"

"Running across a clearing into the large white building down there." Emily pointed down the path.

"The meetinghouse!"

Misi Tomas put his hand on Tama's shoulder. "Misi Sami is on the other side of the plantation with the rest of the students. Go and tell him what has happened. Tell him I have gone to speak with Magale. He will be in charge of school until I get back."

Tama straightened up, took a deep breath, and took off running again—this time farther into the jungle. Misi

Tomas faced the waiting group of boys. They were huddled together, whispering excitedly to one another.

"Go back to the schoolhouse," the missionary told them. "Misi Sami will meet you there with the others. We will continue our work in the plantation tomorrow."

"But, Misi Tomas . . ." one of the taller boys began.

"Go. Go now!" Misi Tomas was firm.

With another long look at Matt and Emily, the boys turned and slipped back into the jungle.

Fiti threaded his long knife into the rope belt around his waist and started to follow the group. But Misi Tomas stopped him.

"Wait, Fiti, you come with me. I may need your help. You, too, Misi Matt and Misi Emi. We must hurry."

Then he headed down the path, with Fiti close on his heels. Matt and Emily hesitated for just a moment.

"Have you figured out what's going on?" Emily said anxiously.

"Are you kidding?" Matt replied. "The only thing I know is that they're not planning on waiting for us. Come on!"

Chapter 4

Matt and Emily raced after them. Misi Tomas led the way, his long legs making short work of the distance. Fiti obviously knew the path so well he could have run it blindfolded. The children quickly learned that if they stayed close behind him and watched what Fiti did, they could avoid tripping on hidden rocks and tree roots or scratching against overhanging branches. But it was not easy. The heat sapped their energy, and when at last they reached the larger clearing, they were panting heavily.

"No sign of anyone yet," Misi Tomas said, glancing around. "Let's hope that means the meeting is still in session."

Fiti looked at Misi Tomas in alarm. "But you cannot walk into a council meeting, Misi Tomas. You are not permitted."

"I know that, Fiti. I'll be breaking all the rules. But if someone doesn't stop Magale, a lot more than rules will be broken. He doesn't understand that he can't treat the United States government like he would treat another tribe. The governor will not stand for it."

"But Magale is our high chieftain," Fiti argued. "He is just as important as the governor."

"Yes, but if the governor hears that the chiefs are uprising, he'll send soldiers to the village and battleships to the beach. If anyone fires a shot, innocent people will be hurt. Buildings could be destroyed. All the American missionaries would be forced to leave. There would be no more school."

"No more school," Fiti echoed in horror. "But what about the students? What would I . . ."

Misi Tomas laid a hand on Fiti's shoulder. "We *will* stop this, Fiti. We must save the school."

He began walking briskly toward the white, wooden building.

Not knowing what else to do, the children followed. As they drew closer, they heard the sound of men's voices— a low rumble of serious conversation. Fiti kept glancing at Misi Tomas, his expression more and more worried the closer they came to the building. Misi Tomas kept his eyes fixed on the open doorway.

"Wait here," he asked, "and pray for me!"

He stepped into the large room. Immediately the talking stopped. The young warriors lining the wooden walls tensed and reached for their weapons, but Misi Tomas ignored them. He approached a group of older men who were sitting cross-legged in a circle in the center of the room. One of the men with wrinkled skin and white hair raised his hand, and the young warriors relaxed their grasps on their knives and clubs.

Misi Tomas faced the old man and bowed his head.

"Your Highness, I know that I am breaking council rules by interrupting your meeting, but I must speak with you. Please, Your Highness. It is most urgent!"

The high chieftain studied Misi Tomas for a few moments before giving a nod and waving his arm toward the other men who surrounded him. "These are the chieftains of our neighboring villages. What you have to say to me may be said before them also."

"Thank you, Your Highness. What I have to say concerns all the chieftains of the island." Misi Tomas paused, choosing his words carefully. "Your Highness, is it true that you are planning to fight the United States government in order to get your way with the governor?"

Magale, the high chieftain, puffed out his chest. "We have made a formal request to the governor which he has refused to consider. Naturally, we are very disappointed. We have decided that if we make a show of force, the governor will see that he cannot deal so lightly with our wishes."

Misi Tomas took a deep breath. "Your Highness, perhaps you have not considered what this will mean to your villages. As soon as the governor finds out about this uprising, he'll send soldiers from Pago Pago to your village and take you and all these other chieftains to jail. What you are planning to do will be considered high treason. You must not go to war against the United States!"

A few whispers passed between the chieftains. Then Magale spoke again.

"You have no need to fear, Misi Tomas. The soldiers will not reach us here at the village. We have some of our warriors lying in wait for them along the road. They will ambush the soldiers with shotguns and kill them. We will be safe here."

"No! No!" Misi Tomas cried. "Your Highness, I beg you. You have to stop this now, before anyone is hurt. If any of those American soldiers are injured or killed, the governor will send out one of the navy warships anchored outside the bay, and it will fire on your village."

"They cannot shoot anything from the ocean that would hurt us here," the high chieftain declared confidently.

Misi Tomas stood with his hands clenched. "Your Highness, a ship like that is called a man-of-war. It can hit a target anywhere it wants. Your village would be torn to pieces. Many innocent people could be killed." He paused, then added, "The mission school might be destroyed, and the American missionary teachers would be forced to leave."

The other chieftains leaned forward, and a low murmuring filled the room. Magale could not ignore it. He tilted his head to one side and listened to the whispered words of the elderly chief at his right. He nodded. Matt and Emily held their breath, praying silently that the chieftains would listen to the missionary and realize that he was as concerned for their people as they were.

After a few moments of silence, the high chieftain spoke. "I believe Misi Tomas was inspired to tell us the right thing to do. We will send runners to call off our waiting warriors."

Matt and Emily slowly let out their breath, and Fiti's shoulders relaxed with relief.

"I have runners to offer you," Misi Tomas told the high chieftain. He turned toward the door. "Children, come here."

Fiti immediately moved forward. Matt and Emily glanced nervously at the long line of warriors then stepped up behind him.

"Your Highness, if you will tell Fiti the location of the waiting warriors, he will guide these young missionaries to them. Misi Matt and Misi Emi will give them your message."

The high chieftain gazed at the three children then waved his arm toward the wall of warriors. "Why should I send these children when my own men stand ready?"

"It is important that these warriors return to their own villages immediately," Misi Tomas explained. "They must not be here when the soldiers arrive. They would be seen as a threat."

Magale gave a pleased smile. "Yes. They are fierce and worthy warriors."

Matt and Emily looked over at the men covered in war paint. Not one moved a muscle as their leader spoke about them. They stood, silently waiting for his command. All at once, the high chieftain clapped his hands.

"To your villages!" he called. "Return to your families through the jungle."

The warriors responded at once. They slipped out through the open door as quickly and quietly as they'd entered. For a few moments, the children heard the men's feet running swiftly across the clearing outside. Then they were gone.

"The other warriors, Your Highness. The ones waiting for the soldiers. We must reach them quickly," Misi Tomas said.

The high chieftain beckoned to Fiti. Fiti took three steps forward and bowed.

"Young Fiti, do you know the Cave of the Flying Foxes?" he asked.

Fiti stood tall. "Yes, Your Highness."

"Four warriors wait there, watching the road. When they see the soldiers coming, they will leave the cave and join six more warriors who wait beside the road at Dolphin Rock. Try to reach the warriors at the cave first. They can warn the others."

"Yes, Your Highness." Fiti bowed again.

The high chieftain looked at Matt and Emily. "You," he said, pointing to Matt. "Come here."

Matt swallowed hard and followed Fiti's example. He took three steps forward and bowed.

"Your name?"

"Misi Matt, Your Highness," Matt replied nervously.

"Come closer, Misi Matt."

Matt took a couple more steps forward until he was within arm's reach of the high chieftain. Magale rose to his feet. He slid a long necklace off his neck and placed it over Matt's head.

"Take this necklace with you, Misi Matt. My warriors will recognize it as a token of trust from Magale, their high chieftain. They will listen to your words."

Matt looked down at the necklace.

Hundreds of tiny shells, shimmering pink, silver, blue, green, and peach, were threaded together in a long chain. One large, polished black shell hung from the center of the chain and rested heavily against his chest. Matt touched the smooth, dark shell.

"Your Highness, you are a leader of courage and integrity," Misi Tomas said. "These children will show similar courage and integrity in trying to reach your warriors. We will pray that they reach them in time. But no matter what happens, it is possible that the governor may still punish you as the leader of this revolt."

The high chieftain slowly nodded. "I understand, Misi Tomas."

"I will stay here with you. When the soldiers come, I will explain your situation and tell them that you voluntarily called off the uprising. I will do

46

everything I can to help your case with the governor."

Again the high chieftain nodded his head. "Thank you, Misi Tomas. When the soldiers come, I will go with them peacefully."

Then he turned to the children and, as he had done before, clapped his hands. "Now go, children. Go quickly. Find my warriors before any blood is shed."

Fiti glanced at Misi Tomas once, then took off running. Matt and Emily didn't even pause. They raced after him, out of the meetinghouse, through the clearing, and into the jungle.

Chapter 5

The children crossed the clearing in seconds. Matt and Emily followed Fiti as he entered the jungle again, this time heading away from the coconut plantation and schoolhouse. The path was narrow, winding back and forth between the tall trees. Dark green vines hung from the tree branches. Large, brightly colored flowers dotted the greenery. The dense leaves cut out a lot of the sunlight, making the pathway cool and damp.

Fiti kept a fast pace. Despite the shade, Matt and Emily were hot and gasping for breath when he finally began to slow down.

"How much farther?" Emily panted.

"We are getting close," Fiti replied, "but the hard part is still ahead."

He pointed over Matt's shoulder, and the children swung around to look. Over to the right, towering high above the tops of the trees, was a tall mountain.

"What?" Matt said, looking blankly at the mountain.

"You're not . . . er . . . you're not saying that we have to climb that, are you?" Emily asked.

"Not all the way to the top. Do you see that rocky ridge about halfway up?"

Again Fiti pointed to the mountain. Matt and Emily tried to follow the direction of his finger.

"The one with a couple of trees to one side?" Emily asked.

"Yes. That is the Cave of the Flying Foxes," Fiti said.

Matt squinted, shading his eyes with his hand as he gazed upward. Once more, he envied Emily her great eyesight. "Show me again."

This time Fiti and Emily both pointed, and Matt spotted a gray slice of mountain that stood out from the carpet of green around it.

"Whoa!" Matt breathed. "That's quite a climb."

"You'd have to be a mountain goat or completely nuts to go up there!" Emily said, a hint of panic in her voice.

"Or be trying to save a village and a school," Fiti reminded her.

Emily opened her mouth to argue, but no words would come. He was right. She glanced at Matt who was staring up at the rocky ridge with an expression of determination on his face. Their assignment was more important than her fear of heights. She knew that if they did their best, Heavenly Father would help them.

"Okay," she said quietly. "Which way?"

Fiti left the main path and disappeared between two trees. Emily and Matt followed. Overgrown bushes blocked their way, and clumps of grass grew along the little-used path. The cries of strange birds filled the air, and rustling sounds in the bushes made Matt and Emily jump. Fiti seemed oblivious to them all. Keeping his eyes focused on the narrow trail, he kept the children moving at a steady jog until the ground finally became so steep that they had to use their hands to keep their balance.

As they climbed higher, the trees began to thin, and the path became rockier. Every once in a while, one of the children would slip on the loose stones, and a cascade of small rocks would roll down the hillside. The sound of the bouncing rocks echoed down the mountain, making Emily cling even tighter to the roots, branches, and boulders as she climbed. When another shower of rocks rolled away beneath her feet, she heard Matt scramble out of the way behind her.

"Emily!" he cried. "One more spray like that and we're trading places."

"It's these flip-flops," she said, not daring to look down until she was on firm ground. "They're sliding out from under my feet all the time."

"Shhh!" Up ahead, Fiti had reached a sharp bend in the path and turned quickly to quiet Matt and Emily. "We have reached the cave."

Matt and Emily froze. Where were the warriors? Were they watching them now, their weapons ready?

Very slowly, Matt took the large, black shell in his hand and raised it up so that the necklace could be easily seen.

"We bring a message from Magale to his warriors," he called out.

The children waited—not moving a muscle. The sun beat down upon them, and a big, black beetle scurried across Emily's fingers. Somehow, she held back a scream. The silence was complete.

"Warriors of Magale!" Matt tried again. "We have an important message for you."

From a tall tree behind them, a bird took off with a flutter of wings. Matt shifted one foot and sent more small rocks rolling off the mountainside. Nothing else stirred.

"Come," Fiti called to them. "We will check the cave."

Matt and Emily scrambled after Fiti. When they rounded the corner, he was waiting for them. He was standing on a wide, rocky ledge with a steep drop-off on one side and a giant boulder on the other.

Matt walked over to where Fiti stood and gazed down at the valley below. "Wow! Check that out!" he whispered.

Cautiously, Emily approached the side of the ledge. She couldn't get too close. It made her legs feel like jelly. But even a few feet from the edge, the view was spectacular.

Immediately below them, the jungle spread out like a huge, green blanket. A little farther off, a few wooden buildings and grassy clearings appeared like patches on the blanket. Beyond all that, lay the ocean—a vast stretch of bright blue that touched the sky on the distant horizon and met the land on a golden sandy beach.

"There's the school." Fiti pointed to a rectangular building surrounded by trees in the distance.

Matt was surprised by how small it appeared. "What's so special about the school?" he asked Fiti. "Why are you and Misi Tomas so worried about losing it?"

"You must not have a school where you are from," Fiti said.

Matt shrugged. "Yeah, we do. Lots of them." In fact, the thought of losing a school sounded pretty good to Matt—especially if it meant getting a longer summer vacation.

"Then you should know that without a school there are many things that we would never learn. The missionaries teach us things that our tribal leaders could not—reading and writing, mathematics, geography, history, and science. Students from all over the island wish to attend the school in Mapusaga." There was a hint of pride in Fiti's voice. "Only the best students are admitted."

"So are you from Mapusaga?" Emily asked.

"I am now," Fiti said. "I was born on the other side of the island, but my parents died three years ago. Missionaries taught me the gospel and arranged for me to attend school in Mapusaga. I live at the school with some of the other students."

"You live at the school?" Matt was stunned.

Fiti nodded. "With Mama Pele. She cares for many of the students. So you see, the school is now my home, and Mapusaga is my village."

"Look," said Emily, pointing out to sea, "there's one of those warships Misi Tomas was talking about."

A large, gray ship was steaming into view, moving toward the village.

Fiti turned and ran back toward the boulder. "Hurry! We must check the cave."

On the other side of the boulder, a long crack ran up the rock face. About six feet tall, it was just wide enough to allow a man through. Fiti disappeared through the hole. Matt and Emily followed.

Inside, it was cold, dark, and damp. The children shivered at the sudden change in temperature, and Emily ran her hands up and down her arms.

The children stood still, waiting for their eyes to adjust to the gloom. Another crack ran across the roof of the cave a few yards farther in. Like a shimmering curtain, light seeped through the gap in the rock, illuminating a small patch of ground and casting eerie shadows against the stone walls. The children inched their way forward, arms outstretched.

"Why does it seem muddy in here?" Emily whispered. "I don't hear any water, but the ground's slippery and slimy."

"I do not think there is any water," Fiti said. "But it could be droppings or discarded fruit."

"Yuck!" Emily peered at him. In the dim light she couldn't see his face well enough to tell if he was teasing her. But he had to be. It would take an army of people eating lunch in the cave to drop this much stuff—and who would want to carry lunch up the hill they'd just climbed?

Matt cupped his hands to his mouth. "Is anybody—"

"No!" Fiti hissed. He grabbed Matt's arm and pulled his hand away from his face.

All at once, a fluttering sound filled the cave. High-pitched squeaks and odd snapping noises—like the champing of small teeth—echoed off the walls.

"What's that?" Emily whimpered, backing up as quickly as she dared.

"It's the flying foxes," Fiti whispered. "Hundreds of them sleep in this cave."

"There's really such a thing?" Matt's voice was hoarse. "I thought it was a made-up creature."

"Of course they're real. They are an important part of our island."

The boys had started backing up too. They were only a couple of feet from Emily when she stepped on something slick. Her foot went out from under her, and she landed on her bottom with a thud.

"Ouch!" she cried.

As her cry bounced and echoed off the cave walls, the champing and squeaking increased in volume. On the roof, hundreds of giant wings began to flap and then dive—wave after wave, sweeping down toward Emily. She saw them coming, screamed, and covered her head with her arms. Up they soared again, circling around for another pass.

"Lie down," Fiti yelled.

Emily flattened herself. Fiti dropped down on top of her, covering her body with his.

"Keep still," he whispered. "They won't hurt you. You have woken them from their sleep, and they're as frightened as you are."

Emily could barely breathe, but she didn't move a muscle. Matt plastered himself against the cave wall, trying to make himself invisible. Like kites, swooping and swirling in the air, the flying foxes continued to circle. At last, a few of them flew out through the crack in the rock. Others flew farther back into the cave, and their angry noises began to fade.

Slowly, Fiti raised himself onto his hands and knees.

"Are you okay?" he whispered to Emily.

Emily pushed herself up. Her arms were shaking. "I've got to get out of here," she said, trying hard not to cry.

Fiti stood, and Matt moved away from the wall. Another flying fox sailed by, and the children froze. It was close enough for them to see its shining, dark eyes, its foxlike snout, and its massive batlike wings. Even the small claws on the front of the wings and hind feet glinted as it passed. But this time, the animal ignored them.

Emily struggled to her feet. Very cautiously, the children inched their way to the cave's entrance and out into the blinding sunlight. Blinking and shading their eyes with their hands, they staggered over to the other side of the ledge and collapsed beside each other.

"That was the worst . . . the worst . . ." Emily couldn't even finish the sentence. She had picked a handful of wide leaves and was using them to wipe the goopy mess off her legs, arms, and swimsuit.

"Fiti, you should have warned us," Matt exclaimed.

"I am sorry. I thought you knew. When we were in Mapusaga, you heard everyone talk of the Cave of the Flying Foxes."

"That's really what those things were? Flying Foxes?"

"Of course," Fiti said. "They are one of the largest native mammals on our island. As you saw, they look like bats— but they are much bigger. Their wing span is about as wide as a man's arm span. They hunt by night and sleep by day. But they are fruit eaters. They never hurt anyone. It is just their great size and ugly faces that frighten people."

Emily shuddered. "I'll never be freaked out by a regular, small, black bat again."

"And you may never smell the same, either," Matt said, wrinkling up his nose.

Emily glared at him, but Fiti smiled. "We will pass a river on the way to Dolphin Rock. Perhaps that will help."

"Where is Dolphin Rock?" Matt asked.

Fiti moved over to the other side of the ledge. "It is hidden by the trees, but you can see the road that passes it from Pago Pago."

A small brown ribbon wound through the trees far below.

"And there are the soldiers!" Emily cried.

Sure enough, they could just make out a troop of men marching along the dirt road. Their rifles, held against their shoulders, glinted in the sunlight.

"The warriors waiting here must have seen them too," Matt said. "They've gone to warn the others."

Chapter 6

Fiti scrambled off the ledge and half ran, half slid down the rocky slope. Matt and Emily were right behind him. The journey down was much faster than the journey up, but by the time they reached the jungle floor again, they were covered in cuts and scrapes.

"The soldiers were less than a mile from Dolphin Rock," Fiti announced. "We will have to cut through the jungle to reach the warriors before the soldiers get there."

Emily swept the back of her hand across her forehead. She was hot, tired, and stinky, and the thought of getting lost in the jungle was not a pleasant one. "Can you find Dolphin Rock without following a path?"

"If we keep the mountain to our right and stay this side of the river, we will meet the road just above Dolphin Rock," Fiti said confidently.

"We don't have a choice, Em," Matt said, whooshing a persistent fly away from his face. "Let's get going."

They plunged into the forest. Fiti took out the knife he'd been using in the coconut plantation and hacked away at the branches, cutting a narrow trail through the undergrowth. Matt and Emily followed, stepping over low bushes and pushing tree limbs out of their way. It was hard to move quickly. Fiti kept glancing to his right, trying to keep track of their distance from the mountain.

"How close are we to the river?" Emily asked. She could hear the sound of running water, but it didn't seem to be getting any nearer.

"With the soldiers so close to Dolphin Rock, we must find the warriors before you wash," Fiti said.

Emily pulled a face. "I don't think I can stand the smell coming from my clothes much longer."

"We've got to keep moving, Em," Matt urged from the back. "You're not so stinky now that all the goop has dried."

"You're not wearing the stink," Emily said miserably.

Fiti stopped to pull back a big branch.

"You will not have to wait long," he said. "The road is very close."

He took a step, then tripped on a protruding root. The branch slipped from his hand, sprang back, and whacked him across the head with a resounding crack. Fiti fell to the ground.

"Fiti!" Matt and Emily cried, dropping to their knees beside the boy. "Fiti, are you all right?"

Fiti groaned and lifted his hand to his head. "Oh, that hurt!"

He shook his head, as though trying to clear it of pain and confusion, then moaned again. Movement seemed to make it worse. He leaned back against the tree and closed his eyes.

"You must go," Fiti said, his eyes still closed. "Leave me here, and come back after you have taken Magale's message to the warriors."

"We can't leave you here all alone," Matt said.

"You have to." Fiti was firm. "Go . . . Go now."

"But we don't know the way," Emily said.

Matt stood up and looked over at the mountain. "Mountain on the right, river on the left."

Fiti nodded, then grimaced in pain. "Yes. It can't be far now. Take my knife. Mark your path. Then you can follow it back to me."

Matt picked up the knife.

"But, Fiti, your head . . ." Emily began.

"Go!" Fiti urged through clenched teeth. "The school. The village. Many, many people will be hurt if you do not hurry."

"Hang in there, Fiti," Matt said. "We'll be back to help you soon."

Matt swung the knife in front of him and cut a branch off the nearest bush. He swung again and disappeared through the tiny gap he'd created in the shrubbery. With a last, worried look at Fiti's pale face, Emily stumbled after her brother.

"Matt," she called. "There's nowhere to kneel down, and we don't have time to stop, so while you mark the path, I'm going to say a prayer."

Matt didn't stop moving for a second. "Pray out loud so I can hear," he called back.

So as they ran, Emily prayed. She prayed for Fiti's safety and their own. She prayed that Matt's good sense of direction wouldn't let them down. She prayed that they'd find Dolphin Rock and the waiting warriors before the soldiers arrived.

Almost as soon as they'd said amen, Matt cut through a thick bush and stumbled onto a narrow dirt road. Emily followed him through and almost landed on top of him.

"You found the road," she gasped. "But which way do we go?"

Matt crouched down and shoved the knife's blade into the dirt beneath the bush. The lowest branches hid it from the road, but it would act as a marker when they needed to find their way back to Fiti. He rose to his feet and paused. He looked left and right.

"Left," he said.

For once, Emily didn't question him. They'd prayed for help. Matt had always had a good sense of direction. They would go left.

They ran down the dirt road in silence. Emily's eyes darted back and forth, searching for any kind of movement among the trees and bushes that lined the path. She noticed Matt doing the same thing. Every little sound startled them, but neither of them saw another person or, for that matter, anything that could be called Dolphin Rock. Their breath was coming out in short gasps, and the pain in Emily's side was getting worse with each step.

"Do you think we should turn back?" Emily panted.

"Not till we've passed the next corner," Matt replied.

They reached the bend in the road and began to slow their steps when suddenly a huge man covered in war paint leapt out from behind a tall tree. He stood right in front of them, his legs apart, one arm raised with a long hooked knife in his hand.

"Who are you? And what are you doing here?" he shouted.

Emily screamed, and Matt clapped his hand over her mouth.

"The soldiers," he hissed.

Emily nodded her understanding, and Matt uncovered her mouth. He took off the necklace that Magale had given him and offered it to the warrior.

"My name is Misi Matt," Matt began. "And this is my sister, Misi Emi. We're missionaries working with Misi Tomas in Mapusaga. The high chieftain, Magale, has an urgent message for his warriors. He said that if we showed you his necklace, you would know that he had sent us."

The large warrior turned the necklace over in his hand then gave a low whistle. From all around, leaves rustled and warriors appeared, dropping out of trees and coming out from behind bushes. They crowded around the first warrior, eyeing the children and then the necklace.

"We don't have much time," Matt urged. "The soldiers are coming. We saw them from the Cave of the Flying Foxes."

"You went to the cave?"

"Yes. Magale told us to go there first. When we realized you'd gone, we guessed you'd seen the soldiers coming and had come to warn the warriors waiting at Dolphin Rock."

"We have only just arrived ourselves. How did you travel so quickly?"

"We cut through the jungle. Fiti, from the village, was our guide."

"I know Fiti," one of the warriors said. "He is from the school at Mapusaga and is an honorable young man."

"He injured his head, and he's waiting not far from the road," Matt explained. "He needs help, but we had to give you Magale's message first."

Emily suddenly tugged on Matt's arm.

"They're coming, Matt! I can hear their footsteps. Hurry!"

The warriors became alert. "To your positions!" whispered the large warrior.

"No! Wait!" Matt's cry checked their movement. "Magale does not want you to ambush the American soldiers. It's vital that no one is injured. He has changed his mind and plans to meet with the governor himself."

"We are not to attack the soldiers?" Disbelief was clear on the warrior's face.

"That's the message," Matt said.

"But we are prepared," the warrior began.

"We know you could do it, but you mustn't!" Emily cried. "You have the high chieftain's necklace as our guarantee. Magale now realizes that your villages will be in terrible danger if any of the soldiers are hurt. He wants all his warriors to return to their villages as quickly and quietly as they can."

They could all hear the marching feet now. The large warrior had to make a decision—and fast.

"To your positions," he whispered again.

"Please!" Emily begged. "You have to believe us!"

The warrior lifted up his hand to silence her. "To your positions—and lie low. No one is to move until the soldiers have passed by."

There was another rustle of leaves, and, as if by magic, the warriors disappeared. The large warrior turned to Matt and Emily. "Dolphin Rock. Quickly!"

The children raced after the large warrior. He led them a few yards farther down the dirt road. And then they saw it—a huge, gray slab of rock jutting out of the ground. High above their heads, the top of the rock arched like a leaping dolphin's back, and a streak of black marked the stone just where the dolphin's eye should be.

The large warrior ducked behind a cluster of fern bushes growing beside the large rock. Then he leaned over and pulled Emily and Matt behind the ferns too. The ferns were so tall that Matt and Emily could stand upright and not see over the tops of the delicate leaves. The large warrior was not so fortunate. Crouching low, he hurried around to the back of Dolphin Rock and leaned against its solid surface. He stood still, his head tilted slightly, listening for the sound of the marching soldiers. Matt and Emily moved closer, leaning their backs against the rock too.

The jungle was silent. The leaves were still. Even the birds had stopped their chattering. Matt and Emily barely dared to breathe. They prayed that the warriors would obey the order to lie low and that the soldiers would pass Dolphin

Rock without even knowing the warriors were watching from the trees.

The marching feet drew nearer, and now the soldiers were close enough that the children could almost feel them. One of the men had a boot that squeaked with every footstep. It was as regular as the ticking of a clock. Someone coughed. At exactly that moment, something dropped onto Emily's head. Instinctively, she reached up. The "something" was squishy and moving.

"Aah!" she cried, lowering her head and swiping her hand across it. A light green gecko flew to the earth and scurried off at top speed.

"That lizard thing was on my head," she whispered in horror, then bit her lip as she realized what she'd done. The large warrior and Matt were not looking at her, but were straining to hear the sounds from the road. The regular marching beat had stopped.

"Who's there?" a man called. "We have guns, and we're prepared to use them."

"Leave through the jungle!" Matt urged the warrior. "We'll go out to meet the soldiers and distract them. We're American children. They won't harm us. But they must not find you here."

Before the warrior could say a word, Matt grabbed Emily's hand and pulled her around Dolphin Rock.

"Make lots of noise," he said. "We can cover the warrior's escape."

He started tromping through the bushes and shouting in English. "Don't shoot! We're coming!"

Emily caught on quickly. As they pushed their way through the tall ferns, she purposely brushed against them, making them swish loudly.

"Ouch! That hurt," she called. "Wait for me!"

Neither of them looked back. They merely hoped the warrior had slipped away. They didn't have time to wander for long. As they emerged from the wall of fern leaves, a dozen American soldiers faced them with rifles cocked and ready.

"Kids!" one of them exclaimed.

"American kids!" added another one.

One by one the rifles lowered.

"Who are you? And what are you doing here?" the first soldier demanded.

Matt stuck out his hand as he'd seen the missionaries do. "I'm Matt Williams," he said. "This is my sister, Emily. We're here to help the Mormon missionaries in Mapusaga."

Confused, the soldier shook Matt's hand. "You're not in Mapusaga."

Emily spoke up. "Someone in Mapusaga told us about the Cave of the

Flying Foxes. It's up there somewhere." She waved in the vague direction of the mountain. "But it's really hard to find your way through the jungle."

He looked Emily up and down. "You look like you've been rolling in the jungle."

Matt had a sudden coughing attack, and Emily's cheeks burned. She wished she could give her brother a swift poke in the ribs.

"I fell," she said.

"Hmm." The soldier eyed the children suspiciously. "We're on our way to Mapusaga. You come with us. We'll see if there's anyone there who can back up your story."

He gave a short command, and immediately the men moved back into organized rows. He pointed his rifle to a small gap in the middle of the soldiers. "Stand there," he commanded.

"You need to keep up with us. And no talking."

Matt and Emily glanced at each other. There was no sound from the jungle. Had the warriors left? And what about Fiti? No one else knew where to find him. They had to get back to him—and soon.

Chapter 7

The officer shouted a command, and, in unison, the soldiers began marching again. Left, right, left, right. Matt and Emily quickly picked up the rhythm. Once, just to see what would happen, Matt stopped marching. Emily stumbled to a halt beside him. But the soldiers did not even pause. The one standing immediately behind Matt gave him a push with the handle of his rifle, and Matt was forced to move forward or be run over.

Matt glanced over at Emily. She was chewing her bottom lip—a sure sign that she was worried. He gave her an encouraging smile. He wasn't worried about their safety. The American soldiers would not harm them. And he was pretty sure that once they met up with Misi Tomas, he'd be able to get them out of this scrape. But they couldn't afford to walk all the way back to the village of Mapusaga. Every step they took down the road led them farther from their friend. They needed to return to Fiti.

Desperately, Matt racked his brain for a way to escape the soldiers. Their escape would certainly frustrate the men, but he was pretty sure that they would not follow them. The soldiers were on a far more important assignment, and their priority would be to continue on to Mapusaga.

He noticed Emily glance to her left. She stumbled slightly, caught herself, then looked to her left again. Could she see something or someone?

Matt gazed at the thick wall of trees and shrubs, then back at Emily. Something was bothering her. What had those radar eyes spotted now?

"Em. What is it?" he whispered.

She gave a tiny shake of her head and kept on marching, her eyes facing forward again. Matt gave the jungle at his side one more look, then faced forward too. It was time to start praying for help.

Before they rounded the bend, they heard the noise—a slow creaking, accompanied by a steady clip-clop. Matt and Emily strained to see what was up ahead, but the soldiers in front of them blocked their view. Minutes later, however, the officer barked another order, and the soldiers began lining up along the edge of the road. In front of them the dirt road ended, and a very narrow wooden bridge began. The bridge was the only way across the deep valley, and at that moment, it was completely blocked.

Standing in the middle of the bridge was a gray horse pulling a small, two-wheeled wooden wagon. Inside the wagon sat a white-haired Samoan woman and a young boy. The boy was shaking the reins, urging the gray horse on, but the horse would not move. The mare had spotted the line of men wearing khaki uniforms and carrying guns, and she refused to get any closer.

Frustrated, the young boy climbed out of the wagon. He grabbed hold of the bridle and yanked hard, pulling the horse forward with all his might. The horse shook her head wildly, shaking the boy along with it. Her feet skittered back and forth then sideways, and the small wagon followed—jolting uncontrollably. There was a terrible groan followed by a shuddering bang as one wheel slipped off the edge of the bridge and the wagon slid onto its axle.

"Help!" the boy cried desperately.

The officer gave an order, and half the soldiers placed their heads through their gun straps and swung their rifles onto their backs. The other soldiers raised and cocked their rifles, watching warily as their comrades moved onto the bridge. The men walked carefully and quietly, trying not to agitate the horse any more than she already was. One soldier extended his hand to the horse and started talking to her in a soft voice.

"Come here, girl," he called. "Come on. Nothing to be afraid of."

Within seconds he was at her side, running his hand down her long neck, petting her and praising her. The horse turned her head, rubbing her nose against the soldier's khaki shirt.

"That's the way. Good girl."

The soldier grasped the bridle in one hand and continued to pet the horse with the other.

"All right, son," he said, using the same steady voice he'd used with the horse. "Slowly, see if you can help your grandma. I'll hold on to your horse."

He gave a slow nod to the other men, and they began inching forward again. They squeezed past the tipped wagon, some on one side and some on the other. With grunts and groans, they began heaving the wheel up and back onto the bridge. The young boy quickly climbed up into the wagon beside his grandmother. He took her hand and patted it reassuringly, while watching the soldiers with anxious eyes.

The soldier with the horse urged her forward. With a quick snort, the horse took one step, then another, then another. There was a loud thud as the men lowered the wheel onto the wooden bridge, and then the creaking wheels began to turn. A few of the soldiers on the bridge gave a subdued cheer.

Emily looked at the soldiers around her. Their eyes were all focused on the wagon and the men now making their way across the bridge. Matt was leaning forward, watching the wagon's progress too. Behind her, a bird called. The horse snorted, and the bird called again. Emily turned around. A pair of eyes peered out at her from the center of a nearby bush. She gasped, then tried to cover it with a cough. She looked back again. This time, a hand appeared between the branches. A finger beckoned.

Carefully, Emily reached out and grabbed the sleeve of Matt's T-shirt. She gave it three sharp tugs. He swung around, and she immediately put her finger to her lips, urging him not to make a sound. Then, without saying a word, she pointed to him, to herself, and then at the bush.

Matt understood at once. He glanced at the soldiers standing on either side of him and took a baby step backwards. No one noticed. He took another step—this time a little bigger. Again, no one noticed.

Emily followed, and within seconds they had both inched their way back onto the road. The damp dirt silenced their footsteps, and the children moved faster, knowing that their only hope was to disappear before the wagon was successfully over the bridge. Emily led the way, guiding Matt to the bush where she'd seen the hand appear. When they reached the bush, it parted before them, and the children stepped back into the jungle.

The large warrior, whom they'd last seen at Dolphin Rock, carefully released the branches he was holding, and instantly the gap closed. He flashed them a smile, and, without a word, the children fell into step behind him.

They had not gone far when they heard the soldiers shouting. Someone had noticed that they were gone. Seconds later there was the unmistakable sound of running feet, followed by the swishing and cracking of branches being pushed apart and broken. The jungle was suddenly alive with people— people who were approaching from every direction. Matt felt a surge of panic. He began to run, but the large warrior stepped right in front of him and held him back.

"No!" he whispered. "There are too many of them. Our best chance of escape is to go up."

The large warrior pointed to a large scrub oak. Its gnarled branches worked their way up the trunk like a giant staircase. The children raced to the tree and started climbing. Higher and higher they went. The warrior followed them up, stopping only when the ground below was hidden by a curtain of leaves.

The sound of men crashing through the jungle surrounded them, but the leaves prevented the children from seeing the soldiers. Instead, Matt focused on a gecko that was running up and down the trunk of the tree. He was prepared to brush it away if it got too close to Emily. He didn't want a repeat of her last gecko experience.

And Emily wouldn't have seen it until it was too late. She was sitting on a branch with her eyes closed, mentally singing one Primary song after another.

The soldiers' heavy footsteps and grumbling voices finally faded into the distance, but long after the jungle became quiet again, the warrior and the children stayed in the tree. Barely daring to breathe, they sat and waited. At last, a bright yellow bird with red-tipped wings flew onto one of the branches of the old oak tree. It perched right above Matt's head and let out a trill song. The Samoan looked up at the bird and smiled.

"That is our sign," he said. "When the birds start singing again, the forest is safe."

He swung himself down from the branch where he'd been sitting, and within seconds he was on the ground.

Matt and Emily followed him down. They were stiff from sitting in the same position for so long. It felt good to be standing again.

"My name is Siatu," he said. "I must thank you for distracting the American soldiers at Dolphin Rock so that my warriors could return to their villages unharmed. Sio, the warrior from Mapusaga, was worried about the boy, Fiti. You said he was injured."

"Yes," Matt said. "We must go back to him as fast as we can."

"Do you remember exactly where you left him?"

"If you can get us to Dolphin Rock, I can find him from there."

Siatu looked pleased. "Sio is waiting at Dolphin Rock. We will meet him there and go with you to find Fiti."

Chapter 8

Matt and Emily never could figure out how Siatu took them directly to Dolphin Rock. They traveled through vine-filled jungle that looked as though no man had ever walked that way before. They saw no markings on the trees or landmarks along the way, but not once did Siatu backtrack or pause to get his bearings.

"I waited until the other warriors were safely on their way to their homes before following you," Siatu said. "It wasn't hard to track a troop of marching soldiers."

"You watched us from the trees, didn't you?" Emily said. "I thought I saw someone."

Siatu smiled. "You have good eyes, little one."

"She has weird eyes," Matt said grumpily.

Siatu laughed. "I was grateful for her eyes when I needed your attention at the bridge, but it is your golden hair that all islanders admire."

Matt ran his hand through his blond hair. "Well, it's not very useful, and it never does what I want it to do."

"Maybe so." The large warrior gave Matt an encouraging pat on the back. "But we will depend upon *you* to lead us to Fiti."

Siatu put his hands to his mouth and blew gently. The warbling call of a bird floated through the air. Seconds later, they heard another call—a perfect echo of Siatu's. The large warrior looked pleased.

"It is Sio," he said. "He is waiting at the rock. All is clear."

They reached Sio minutes later. He was hidden in a grove of trees beside Dolphin Rock. He greeted Siatu warmly.

"You were successful," he said, glancing at the children.

"Thanks to an old gray horse," Siatu replied.

Sio raised his eyebrows questioningly, but Siatu didn't take the time to explain. "Misi Matt says he can lead us to Fiti. The boy has been alone for too long. We must hurry."

Matt and Emily stepped over to the side of the dirt road. They paused, listening for any sound of someone approaching. There was none. So they took off up the road, glad to be able to run free from branches, shrubs, and vines. When they rounded the bend in the road, Matt slowed his pace to a gentle jog. He studied each bush as he passed, looking for the drooping branches that hid Fiti's knife.

"Over here!" he called, catching a glint of metal between some leaves. He lifted the branches, and there it was—the blade buried just where he'd left it.

He pulled the knife out of the damp earth and wiped the blade on the broad leaves of a bush. Siatu pushed back the branches and stepped into the jungle. Sio and the children followed.

"Which way?" Siatu asked.

Matt pointed to his right. "We need to head that way. I left marks on many of the bushes and trees. We should be able to follow them straight to Fiti."

They hurried forward in single file, with Matt leading the way. He found it quite easy to follow the trail of lopped-off limbs and trampled undergrowth, and they made good time. They soon reached a tiny clearing where the ground cover was flattened in an irregular oval shape.

"This is it," Matt said. "This is where we left him."

Emily looked down at the crushed plants at the feet of an ancient sycamore tree. "He was sitting right here," she said, chewing her bottom lip anxiously. "His head hurt so much that he couldn't even stand up. Where could he be?"

The two Samoans walked around the small clearing, studying the ground and the bushes.

"There is no sign of blood," Siatu told them.

Emily shook her head. "He had a red mark across his forehead, but he wasn't bleeding."

Sio pointed to a bush with broken branches. "Is this the way you came from the Cave of the Flying Foxes?"

"Yes," Matt said.

"I think he must have gone back the same way. There are only two places where the vegetation has been disturbed—the way we came from the road, and the way you came from the cave. Unless he left the path you marked, we would have seen him. He must have tried to return the way he came."

"Maybe he thought we weren't going to come back for him," Emily said miserably.

Siatu shrugged. "That is not important now. We must focus all our energy on finding him. We will try following the path you took from the

Cave of the Flying Foxes, but we must also watch for signs that he left the trail." He looked down at the children, his expression grave. "This is the time we really need your eyesight, Misi Emi, and your sense of direction, Misi Matt."

"Let's go," Matt said. "We're wasting time."

Once again, he led the way onto the trail. Siatu followed him, with Emily and Sio bringing up the rear. Matt and Siatu focused on watching for the trail marks. Emily and Sio scoured the bushes and trees for any sign that Fiti may have passed that way. The jungle was full of noises—the buzzing of insects, the chattering of small animals, and the song of many birds. But they didn't hear anything that could have been Fiti.

Every once in a while, Emily would call out his name, pause, and listen for a reply. The only response she ever received was a moment of silence in the jungle sounds. Then nature's chorus would begin again, and Emily would walk on a few more yards.

They'd been traveling like this for some time when Emily suddenly stopped. Sio ran right into her.

"What is it, Misi Emi?" he said.

Emily ran her hands up and down her arms. It was hot and humid, but she had goose bumps. "I don't know," she said. "But something . . . there's something . . ."

She pivoted around slowly, looking and listening hard. There was a new sound. A faint, gurgling, bubbling sound.

"Listen," she whispered. "Do you hear it?"

Matt and the two Samoans concentrated on the noises around them.

"Water," said Sio. "There is water running nearby."

He took a step to the left and touched a bush with bright yellow flowers. "Look!" He pointed to the ground. A handful of yellow petals was scattered on the dirt. "These petals are not from a dying flower. They are healthy and full of life—and they fell very recently."

Siatu pointed to a fern frond beside the flowering bush that was bent in half.

"Something—or someone—passed by here not too long ago."

He stepped over the bush and studied the ground. "This way," he said.

As Siatu followed the faint trail of broken twigs and bent grass, the sound of running water became more and more distinct. At last, Siatu pushed aside a young sapling and entered another small clearing. The ground was muddy and covered in paw prints of every shape and size. A tiny spring of water was bubbling up through a crack in a large boulder. The water ran down the face of the rock and trickled onto the ground in a meandering ribbon. Muddy puddles dotted the area. Lying facedown beside the largest puddle was a boy.

"Fiti!" Matt and Emily cried in unison.

They ran forward, kneeling down in the mud beside their friend. The two Samoans crouched down on either side of Fiti's body.

"Is he . . . is he dead?" Emily turned her fearful eyes toward Siatu.

Siatu placed his fingers on Fiti's neck and bent down until his face was within inches of the boy's.

"His pulse is weak, but he is breathing," Siatu announced. "We must get him to the village."

"He needs a priesthood blessing," Emily said softly. She looked up at the two Samoans. "Do either of you hold the priesthood?"

Siatu looked at her blankly, but Sio nodded solemnly.

"I am an elder," he said.

"An elder?" Siatu questioned him. "What do you mean?"

"I belong to The Church of Jesus Christ of Latter-day Saints . . ."

"Is that the church that runs the school in Mapusaga?" Siatu interrupted.

"Yes. I was baptized with my mother and sister four years ago, and I was given the Melchizedek Priesthood and made an elder in the Church last year. Because of the priesthood I hold, I can give Fiti a special blessing."

Siatu then looked on with amazement as Sio placed his hands on Fiti's head, bowed his own head, and began to pray. He blessed Fiti with health, strength, and a full recovery. When Sio said amen, Matt released a long breath that he hadn't even realized he was holding. Emily looked down on Fiti with tears in her eyes.

"He'll be okay now," she whispered.

Siatu opened his mouth as though he were about to say something, and then he promptly closed it again. He leaned over and, gently supporting Fiti's head, turned the boy onto his back. The red line still marked Fiti's forehead, but it was now surrounded by swollen purple skin. His left eyelid was also swollen, so when his eyelids began to flutter, only one eye opened completely.

Fiti stared at the large warrior in dazed confusion. Siatu, still covered in war paint, was a frightening sight.

"Fiti," Emily called.

The boy slowly turned his head to face her. He winced in pain at the movement.

"Fiti, it's Misi Emi and Misi Matt. We've brought Siatu and Sio to help you back to the village."

Fiti ran his tongue over his dry lips. "I thought you were not coming back." His voice cracked. "I waited until the sun was lowering in the sky. But I had to . . ." He swallowed hard. "I had to find water."

Sio moved closer. In his hand he held a large leaf that he'd folded into the shape of a cup. He'd filled it half full with water from the spring. Very carefully, he raised the leaf cup to Fiti's lips and poured the spring water, a few drops at a time, into his mouth.

"We will get you to the village," he told Fiti. "Mama Fiu'u will help you feel better very soon."

Fiti closed his eyes again. "Yes," he said. "Mama Fiu'u will know what to do."

Chapter 9

Siatu instructed Matt to kneel down behind Fiti, and he gently rested the boy's head on Matt's knees. Emily took charge of Sio's leaf cup and made sure she had fresh spring water ready whenever Fiti asked for it. The two men got to work cutting down tree branches, vines, and huge leaves from the palm trees. The Samoans worked quickly and efficiently. In a matter of minutes, they had constructed a stretcher with a long branch on either side lashed together with vines. The sturdy palm tree leaves were woven in and out of the vines to create a covering for Fiti to lie on.

"If Sio and I help you, do you think you can stand?" Siatu asked Fiti when the stretcher was ready.

"I will try," Fiti replied bravely.

Siatu nodded, pleased with the boy's reply. "He is ready, Sio."

But Sio was kneeling on the ground a few yards away, his ear up against a fallen log. As the children watched, he raised his head and cut a chunk off the log. Then he put his ear to the log again and chopped off most of the other end.

"What's he doing?" Emily asked.

"If we are lucky, he has found something good to eat," Siatu said. "Sio has a talent for finding the exact spot in the wood."

Mystified, Matt and Emily continued to watch as Sio carefully cut into the log on each side and, at last, lifted out a big, fat, wiggling woodworm. With a broad smile, he rose to his feet, the white, four-inch-long woodworm dangling on the end of the knife.

"Would you like to eat this delicious woodworm, Misi Emi?" he asked.

Emily looked at him in horror. Was he serious?

"I . . . uh . . . I'm actually not very hungry right now," she managed to say.

"Misi Matt? It is a delicacy of the Samoan jungle." He offered the woodworm to Matt.

"Thanks, Sio," Matt said most politely. "I actually ate some gummy worms this morning, and I think Fiti is the one who needs it the most."

"Gummy worms," Sio repeated with interest. "I have not heard of the gummy worm. I do not believe it is found on our island. Fiti, the young missionaries would like you to have the delicious woodworm. You are honored."

He plucked the woodworm off the end of the knife and handed it to the Samoan boy. Fiti held the woodworm between his fingers.

"Thank you, Misi Matt and Misi Emi. You are very kind," he said humbly. Then he bit off one end of the woodworm, chewed it slowly, and swallowed.

"Oh, gross!" Emily had her hand over her mouth. "I think I'm going to be sick."

Matt's face was a picture of disbelief. "Nasty!"

The Samoans chose to ignore Matt's and Emily's reactions to the woodworm. Fiti savored every bite. Once he'd finished it completely, he thanked Sio again.

"It was truly delicious. Thank you, Sio."

"I am glad that you enjoyed it, young Fiti. Now we should be on our way."

The two men positioned themselves on either side of the young Samoan. On the count of three, they raised the boy to his feet. Fiti staggered sideways, and they held him steady, waiting for him to regain his balance. Then, very slowly, they walked him to the stretcher and helped him lie down on the palm leaves.

"It's going to be a bumpy ride," Siatu warned. "But it will be a lot easier than making you walk or carrying you on our backs."

"Thank you," Fiti murmured. "I promise I will not complain."

Siatu laughed. "Ah, you can tell Sio to treat you more carefully as often as you like."

Sio smiled good-naturedly. "Only if it takes your mind off the pain in your head."

Siatu and Sio took their places at each end of the stretcher and carefully lifted it up. The vines stretched and creaked under Fiti's weight, but they held.

"Misi Matt," Siatu called. "You go ahead. You and Misi Emi must clear the way for us. Cut or hold back the branches so that Sio and I can pass through with the stretcher. We will go back to the trail we were following. We must keep the mountain to our left and walk away from the setting sun. It will not take us long to reach the sea, and we can follow the beach to Mapusaga. It will be easier to walk along the sand than through the jungle, and it will keep us away from the soldiers on the road. If we make good time, we can still reach the village before the soldiers do."

With Fiti's knife in his hand, Matt started out. He only had to check their course direction once with Siatu. Otherwise, he led them as well as a seasoned warrior. Before very long, the sounds of the jungle were replaced with the cries of seagulls and the rhythmical swish of ocean waves.

Finally, they emerged at the edge of the jungle. Huge, broken boulders of ancient lava rock lay at their feet in a tumbled mass. Beyond the rocks was a vast expanse of sparkling white sand. And then, for as far as the eye could see, lay the bright blue ocean. For a few moments Matt and Emily simply stared.

"It's so . . . so . . . big!" said Matt, failing to find a word that could describe his first close-up view of the sea.

"It's amazing!" Emily said.

"Yeah, that too," Matt agreed.

Puzzled, the two Samoan men looked at each other and then at the scene before them.

"It looks much as it usually does," Siatu said.

"But it is beautiful," Sio hastened to add. "Particularly at the end of the day."

The breeze blowing off the ocean puffed the loose wisps of Emily's hair away from her face. Matt closed his eyes and took a deep breath. The air smelled of salt.

"We must keep moving," Siatu reminded the children. The two men had not once put Fiti down to rest their arms. "Crossing the boulders will be one of our biggest challenges. Fiti, my friend, hold on tight."

Obediently, Fiti wrapped his fingers around the branches and braced himself for a bumpy ride. Even though Siatu was taller than Sio, the men did their best to keep the stretcher level. Barefoot, they slowly made their way up, down, and around the barrier of boulders.

At last, the large boulders became smaller rocks, and the gravelly ground gave way to smooth sand. Matt and Emily took off their flip-flops and ran along the water's edge.

A little farther down the beach, an outcrop of boulders jutted into the sea, and the sandy beach all but disappeared. The Samoans did not let it slow them down, however. Holding the stretcher high, they waded through the knee-deep water, with Matt and Emily close behind. Almost immediately, a piece of seaweed wrapped itself around Matt's ankle. He hopped on one foot, trying to free himself of the slimy plant—and didn't even notice the wave rolling toward him. Emily tried to call out a warning, but it was too late. One second, Matt was upright. The next second, he was sitting up to his armpits in salty water.

"Argh!" Matt cried.

Emily burst out laughing. Siatu and Sio looked back and grinned. Even Fiti, who couldn't see Matt from the stretcher, but who had heard the loud splash, smiled.

"Good thing you've got your swimsuit on," Emily teased.

Matt stood up and braced himself for the next wave. "Yeah, well I'm not the one who needed a wash, remember?"

He gave her a shove and down she went.

"Matt!" she spluttered, emerging from the water, wet from head to toe.

"Good thing you've got your swimsuit on," he taunted, and he started to run.

He sloshed his way around the huge boulders and ran back onto the sand. Emily was close behind him, but so were the men carrying the stretcher.

"Shh!" Siatu warned the children. "From now on, we can be seen from the village. We must be careful in case the soldiers have already arrived."

Matt and Emily looked down the beach. The trees grew all the way to the sand along the crescent-shaped bay. Halfway around the bay, there was a clearing in the jungle where several round huts had been built. A plume of smoke curled into the sky, coming from a fire somewhere behind the huts. A few children played in the sand. Three men were hauling a small fishing boat up the beach from the sea, and two women in colorful dresses were standing together beside one of the huts.

"I don't see any sign of the soldiers," Matt said. He looked at Emily to check that she hadn't seen something he'd missed, but she shook her head.

"They would go directly to the meetinghouse," Sio explained. "We cannot see that building from here. It is closer to the coconut plantation."

"Along with the school," Emily guessed.

Sio nodded. "Yes, but Mama Fiu'u lives in the hut closest to the beach."

"I hope she's there," Emily said, looking worriedly at Fiti's pale face.

"It is time for the women to prepare the evening meal. If she is not in her hut, she will be close by."

They had not walked much farther when the village children noticed them coming. They began running down the beach toward them, and the fishermen stopped what they were doing to watch.

"Quickly, children," Siatu called to them. "Run back and find Mama Fiu'u. Tell her we have a boy from the school who needs her medicine."

The village children stared at Matt's and Emily's strange clothes and hair and at the Samoan warriors' painted skin. Without a word, they turned and ran back the way they had come.

"Will they do it?" Matt asked.

"We will soon find out," Sio said. "We may have scared them into it."

"But what if the soldiers are already in the village?" Emily was still watching for any sign of men in khaki uniforms.

"They are not there yet," Siatu said confidently. "If there were soldiers in the village, there would be no children playing on the beach. The soldiers would be much more interesting to watch."

Siatu was right. As the two warriors approached the village carrying the stretcher, the village children reappeared. Behind them were several adults, all hurrying to see what had caused so much excitement among the children.

"Mama Fiu'u," Sio called.

The crowd parted and a short, elderly lady shuffled forward. Her gray hair was pinned up on her head in a long coil. Her skin was as brown and wrinkled as a walnut, but her dark eyes were bright.

"Who is asking for me?" she said, her voice gruff with age.

"It is I, Sio of Mapusaga. Misi Matt, Misi Emi, and Siatu, a worthy warrior from our neighboring village, are returning the young boy Fiti to his village. Fiti has injured his head and is in need of Mama Fiu'u's medicine."

"Let me see the boy," Mama Fiu'u said.

The men lowered the stretcher so that Mama Fiu'u could see Fiti. She placed a gnarled hand on Fiti's cheek and studied the purple swelling now covering half his forehead and left eye.

"Take him to my hut," she said. Then turning to Matt and Emily, she added, "I will need nonu leaves."

"What?" Matt said slowly.

Mama Fiu'u gave him an impatient look. "Children," she called. "Take these young missionaries to the edge of the jungle. Show them where to find the nonu tree."

"Come!" One of the little girls beckoned to Matt and Emily. "We will show you."

Five village children took off, and Matt and Emily hurried after them. The brilliant sunshine had already dried their wet hair and clothes, so they were grateful to enter the shady cover of the jungle again. Immediately, the village children spread out, hunting for the right tree. At last a little boy called out excitedly.

"Here! Over here! "

The other children raced to join him and crowded around the tree. The nonu tree was about eight feet high with a thin trunk and a bushy top of dark green, waxy leaves. Among the leaves were tiny white flowers and bumpy oval fruit about the size of Ping-Pong balls. The fruit varied in color from green to yellow to white.

Matt jumped up and plucked a white fruit from the tree. He pulled a face.

"Yuck!" he said. "It smells awful!"

The village children laughed.

"It is used for medicine," the little girl said, "not for its smell or its flavor."

"You'd better not tell them that your medicine tastes like bubble gum, cherry, or grape," Emily whispered.

126

Matt grinned. He pointed to one of the young boys. "If I give you a piggy-back, could you reach the leaves?"

"Of course," the young boy said, and he was on Matt's back in a second.

Lifting the boy as high as he could, Matt walked closer to the tree.

The young boy showered the waiting children with leaves. They ran to catch them and had gathered them all by the time the boy hopped off Matt's back. Emily stuffed leaves into her pockets. Matt held up the bottom of his T-shirt, and the children filled it with leaves. When they'd finished, he rolled up his shirt one more time to prevent anything from falling out, and they headed back to the village.

As they reached the edge of the jungle a tall, thin boy came into view. He was sprinting across the sand toward them.

"Hurry!" he shouted while still out of breath. "The soldiers have passed the school. They will reach the meeting-house in minutes."

The village children scattered, running like the wind to their family huts. Matt and Emily didn't need to stop and think. They clutched their precious loads and tore after them.

Chapter 10

All the homes in the village were circular. Wooden pillars stood around each building to support the tall roofs. The roofs themselves were made of woven strips of wood, covered with a layer of palm tree leaves. They looked like enormous coconut shells. There were no doors or windows on the huts, just open spaces between the pillars. A few families had lowered woven mats between some of the pillars to create outside walls.

The hut closest to the beach had many of its woven mats lowered. As

Matt and Emily drew nearer, they could not see inside, but they recognized Siatu's voice.

"We must leave, Mama Fiu'u. The soldiers must not see us in our war paint."

"I understand. I will take care of the boy until Mama Pele comes."

Matt and Emily ran around the house. With no door, they weren't sure which side was the front or even how to enter. There was nowhere to knock.

"Mama Fiu'u!" Matt called.

Immediately, one of the woven mats rose. Sio stood beside the pillar.

"I am glad you have come," he said. "Siatu and I must go."

Siatu joined Sio at the pillar. He took off the shell necklace that Matt had given him with Magale's message and placed it back around Matt's neck.

"You are responsible for returning this to Magale, the high chieftain,"

Siatu said solemnly. "Tell him that his warriors did his bidding."

Matt fingered the large black shell that hung at the center of the necklace. "I'll give it to him," he promised.

"Did you bring the nonu leaves?" Mama Fiu'u's voice reached them from across the room.

"Yes," Emily replied.

"Bring them to me," the old woman said.

Matt and Emily turned to say good-bye to Siatu and Sio, but they'd already disappeared.

Fiti was lying on a mat on the floor. His eyes were closed.

"He is sleeping now," Mama Fiu'u said, "but we must be ready when he wakens. The leaves go in the large pot."

Emily emptied her pockets, and Matt unrolled the bottom of his T-shirt. They brushed the leaves into the waiting metal pot. The leaves floated in about an inch of water.

"Very good." Mama Fiu'u nodded her approval. "Now take this pot out to the fire that the women have prepared. The leaves must boil until they are soft. Watch them closely. When they are ready, bring the pot back to me."

"But the soldiers . . ." Emily began.

"Phooey!" Mama Fiu'u brushed the soldiers aside with a wave of her hand. "If they question you, I will tell them you are guests in my house."

"*If* they question us?" Matt whispered to Emily. "Do you get the feeling that Siatu and Sio forgot to tell Mama Fiu'u about our run-in with the soldiers?"

"Yeah. But I also get the feeling that she'd say the same thing anyway," Emily said.

"Right. Well, we'd better start hoping that the fire's really hot and that nonu leaves get soft fast."

It took both Emily and Matt to haul the pot to the fire in the center of the village. Three women were tending the blaze and looked up as the children approached.

"We've brought Mama Fiu'u's nonu leaves," Emily explained.

"Very good." One of the women took the pot from the children and slid the handle onto a metal bar that hung over the fire pit. Using a thick stick, she gently pushed the pot until it sat over the center of the fire.

"The fire is hot. The water will boil quickly," she said. "Why don't you sit and wait with us."

That was just about the last thing Matt and Emily felt like doing. They both thought that running and hiding was a much better idea. But Mama Fiu'u had asked them to watch the pot of leaves, and they couldn't abandon Fiti a second time. Reluctantly, they crouched down beside the fire, but they kept their ears alert for the sound of marching feet—ready to make a dash for it if they had to.

Beside them, the women got back to work. They talked together, gossiping about village life. Every once in a while one of them would glance over at the dirt path that led to the meetinghouse, but their constant chatter and their watchful eyes didn't slow the women's hands at all. Matt watched them for a short time, then couldn't contain his curiosity anymore.

"What are you doing?" he asked.

"Preparing food for the village," one of the women replied.

"The *whole* village?" Emily asked, her eyes wide.

"Of course," the woman said. "Every day we share the fire, we share the preparation, and we share the food."

"Is that today's dinner?"

"Yes. Fresh fish." The woman looked pleased. "It was a good catch today."

"How do you cook it?" Matt asked.

The woman eyed him strangely. "The same way we have cooked it for generations. Have you never seen it done this way before?"

"No," Matt and Emily answered together.

"Then it is time you learned," the oldest woman said. "Come closer."

The children got up and stood beside the woman. She smoothed out a large leaf then took a piece of fish from a bowl and placed it on the leaf. Folding up the sides of the leaf, she wrapped the fish in a tidy bundle and added it to the many other bundles on the floor beside her. Then she turned and pointed to the fire.

"The boys and young men gather the wood and dried coconut leaves. They stack the wood in a cone shape and fill the middle with the coconut fronds. When the heat from the burning fronds has lit the wood, the men put a pile of rocks on the fire. The rocks get very hot, and we scatter them about with a thick pole. We cover the rocks with a layer of banana leaves, and then we put the wrapped-up food on top. We put more banana leaves, more hot rocks, and wet sacks on top of the food to hold in the heat. It makes the hottest oven you can imagine."

The children could see the rocks scattered around in the fire pit.

"Are you ready to put the first layer of banana leaves on now?" Matt asked.

The woman nodded. "As soon as your pot has boiled, we will move it out of the way and begin cooking the fish."

Right on cue, the water in the large pot started to boil. Hissing steam filled the air.

"Watch it carefully, now," one of the other women warned. "The leaves must be softened, but the pot must not boil dry."

Matt inched closer to the pot, waving the steam out of his face so that he could peer inside.

"There's not much water left," he said with concern.

The oldest woman nodded. "It is ready."

She reached for the pot's handle with the long pole and slowly slid it off the metal bar and onto the dirt floor beside the fire pit.

"Take these leaves," she said, handing Matt and Emily some banana leaves. "Wrap them around the handle to protect your hands, and carry the pot back to Mama Fiu'u. She will be waiting for you."

Matt and Emily lifted the pot together. It was hot, but they held the handle at arm's length and walked as quickly as they could to Mama Fiu'u's hut. They only had to stop once to rest their arms before they placed the pot at Mama Fiu'u's feet.

"You have done well," she said, looking into the pot.

She scooped the leaves out and spread them on a clean cloth. Then she shuffled over to Fiti.

"Are you ready, young Fiti?"

"Yes, Mama Fiu'u."

"Sheesh," Matt whispered, looking at the boiled leaves. "That stuff looks awful. I feel really sorry for you, buddy."

Fiti managed a weak smile. "It will help me feel better."

Mama Fiu'u fixed Matt with a crusty glare. "There is an old Samoan saying that says, 'The strangers' treatments will work for the strangers' illnesses, and the Samoan treatments for the Samoan illnesses.' Now, let Fiti rest. I will apply the leaves."

Emily passed Mama Fiu'u the cloth covered with soggy leaves. Mama Fiu'u took the leaves and, one by one, laid them across Fiti's swollen forehead and eye. By the time she'd finished, it looked like half his face was covered in a dark green mask.

"Now you rest and we wait," Mama Fiu'u said calmly.

"Thank you, Mama Fiu'u," Fiti said. He reached out and grasped

Matt's arm. "And thank you, Misi Matt and Misi Emi. Back there in the jungle—you probably saved my life."

"Then we're even," Emily said. "Back there at the Cave of the Flying Foxes—you probably saved my life too!"

"But what about the soldiers? The school? Did we save the . . ."

"This is the United States Army," a loud American voice called. "We've been told to search all the huts in the village."

The three children jumped. Matt and Emily looked at each other in horror. The soldiers had reached the village.

Chapter 11

Unlike Matt and Emily, Mama Fiu'u didn't even flinch when she heard the brusque American voice. She shuffled toward the entrance of her house.

"What are you searching for, soldiers?"

"Warriors who may have gone into hiding."

Mama Fiu'u clicked her tongue. "No warriors here—only children. One injured. Two helping me."

"I'm sorry, ma'am, but our orders are to search every house. We'd like to take your word for it, but that wouldn't do for our superior."

"Very well." Mama Fiu'u shuffled back toward the waiting children. "See for yourself."

There was no place to hide. No bulky furniture. No tables, chairs, beds, or curtains. Nothing. Matt and Emily stood beside Fiti's mat and faced the soldiers as they entered.

The two men blinked as their eyes adjusted from the bright sunlight outside to the dim light inside. First their eyes settled on Fiti, lying on the mat, his face half covered in wet green leaves. Then they noticed the two children standing sentinel beside him.

"Hey," one cried. "You're the kids we lost on the way down here."

The other one stepped forward immediately, grasped Matt and Emily by the arms, and pulled them toward him.

"What are you doing here?" he growled.

Mama Fiu'u fixed him with a fierce glare. "I have already told you. These children have been helping me. Young Fiti was in need of strong medicine from the jungle. I needed Misi Matt and Misi Emi to gather the nonu leaves."

The soldier looked suspicious. "Is that right? Well, what was that story you spun us about the Cave of the Flying Foxes?"

"We did go to the Cave of the Flying Foxes," Emily cried. "That was how Fiti got hurt. We had to run away when you soldiers stopped at the bridge. We'd left Fiti in the jungle, and we knew he needed help. We couldn't wait for the bridge to clear."

"And how did you get back here so fast?"

"We cut through the jungle until we reached the beach," Matt replied. "It was much quicker than taking the road."

The soldiers were not convinced. "And you made that kind of time with an injured boy?"

Matt looked him right in the eye. "Yes, sir."

The soldiers exchanged glances. The one not holding on to Matt and Emily stepped closer to Fiti and looked down at him. Fiti was still lying on the mat. The one eye not covered by leaves was closed. He appeared to be sleeping—but Matt and Emily were pretty sure he was just trying to avoid having to answer any questions.

"What's wrong with the boy?" the soldier asked.

"He hit his head," Mama Fiu'u answered. "His forehead and eye are badly swollen."

"Show me!" the soldier ordered.

Mama Fiu'u pursed her lips together. "It is not time to take off the nonu leaves."

"You don't need to take them off. Just lift them enough for me to see his injury."

Mama Fiu'u tried giving the soldier her crusty glare, but he was as good at looking fierce as she was. Finally, with a grunt of disgust, Mama Fiu'u bent over Fiti and gently pulled up one corner of the leaf covering. The purple, swollen skin beneath was obvious.

"Now you can be satisfied and you can leave," Mama Fiu'u said firmly. "Fiti must rest."

"Thank you, ma'am" the soldier said. "We're sorry to have bothered you." He pointed at Matt and Emily, who were still being held by the other soldier. "You two, however, will accompany us to our superior officer. You can tell *him* your story."

"They have done nothing wrong," Mama Fiu'u protested.

"That may well be the case, ma'am," the soldier said. "But that's for our superior to decide. Not us."

He gave Mama Fiu'u a salute then signaled for the other soldier to exit first, with Matt and Emily in tow. They marched across the clearing and past the large fire pit where the village dinner was now cooking. The women who had helped Matt and Emily with the nonu leaves stopped what they were doing and watched in silence. The soldiers escorted them onto the dirt road that led to the meetinghouse.

It was not long before they saw the long, white building standing on the other side of the clearing. Soldiers were positioned every few yards around the meetinghouse. Standing behind them were small groups of villagers who were watching every move the soldiers made with anxious eyes. In front of the meetinghouse stood the chieftains. Magale, the high chieftain, stood a few steps ahead of the other chiefs. At his elbow was Misi Tomas. They were talking to the American commanding officer.

As the two soldiers approached with Matt and Emily, the discussion stopped. Misi Tomas gave the children a relieved smile. Magale glanced at the necklace around Matt's neck and acknowledged the children with a small nod of his head. The children, in turn, bowed before him.

"Colonel Barrett, sir," the soldier said. "We checked the huts in the village for warriors. We found none. However, we did find these children in the home of the village medicine woman. They claim they were helping her with an injured boy. We thought you might want to question them yourself."

"Thank you, soldiers. Take a position around the clearing."

The two soldiers saluted and retreated to the edge of the clearing. The colonel eyed the children gravely.

"You have some explaining to do," he said. "Your appearance on the road to Mapusaga was suspicious. Your subsequent disappearance cost my men a great deal of time. And now you reappear here—at a time of critical importance. What do you have to say for yourselves?"

Matt shut his eyes for a second. *Please, Heavenly Father,* he begged silently. *Help me know what to say.*

Tell the truth. The feeling came so strongly. *Tell the truth.* Matt looked over at Emily and then Misi Tomas. Misi Tomas caught his gaze and nodded.

Emily gave him an encouraging smile. They'd felt it too. Matt took a deep breath and began to speak.

"My sister and I came to Mapusaga to help the Mormon missionaries. We hadn't been here very long when we found out that the high chieftain, Magale, was pretty mad at the governor. He was thinking about sending his warriors to cause trouble for the governor—because he was tired of being ignored."

Matt glanced at Magale. He stood tall and proud, looking regal with his impressive ceremonial robes and many necklaces. It was hard to imagine anyone ignoring the high chieftain. Beside him, the colonel looked quite insignificant. But Matt sensed his impatience and hurried on.

"Misi Tomas went into the chieftains' meeting. He told them that if they tried to fight to solve their problems with the governor, many innocent people would be hurt. After Misi Tomas had explained the way things work under American law, the high chieftain decided to call off the uprising. But some of the warriors had already left the meetinghouse. So Fiti, my sister, and I were sent to take Magale's message to his warriors. We knew we had to get it to them fast . . ."

Matt paused. He suddenly realized that he had everybody's attention. This was the first time that Misi Tomas, Magale, or the other chieftains had heard what happened.

"On the way, Fiti hit his head on a branch. He couldn't keep going, so he sent us on without him. We met up with the warriors just a few minutes before we met you."

The colonel's eyes never left Matt's face. "And so when we took you both with us, your job was already done?"

"Yes," Matt agreed. "But we'd left Fiti in the jungle. We had to get back to help him. So when your soldiers had to stop at the bridge, we used the distraction to escape and run back to Fiti."

"You did that alone?"

Matt took a deep breath. "Well, actually, a couple of warriors helped us. We couldn't have made it without them. They were the ones who carried Fiti to the village."

"And where are those warriors now?" The colonel's voice was icy.

"They've gone back home to their families."

There was a moment of complete silence. In his mind, Matt was praying again. And he knew Emily and Misi Tomas were too.

"I don't make a habit of believing everything young boys tell me," the colonel began. "In fact, I rarely believe everything most men tell me. But for some reason, I believe you, Misi Matt."

Beside him, Matt heard Emily breath a huge sigh of relief. Misi Tomas smiled. Magale, the high chieftain, said nothing, but Matt got the feeling he was pleased.

"Thank you, sir," Matt said.

"It appears that my men's safe arrival in Mapusaga is due largely to you and your sister. On behalf of the United States military, I thank you."

The colonel saluted him. Matt wasn't sure what he was supposed to do in return, so he smiled at the officer and turned to Magale once more.

"Your Highness," he said, drawing the shell necklace over his head. "Siatu, the warrior, asked me to return this to you and to tell you that your warriors have done your bidding."

Magale took the necklace from Matt's outstretched hands and placed it back around his own neck. Then he put his hand into a small cloth bag that was tied to a belt around his waist. He took something out and pressed it into Matt's hand.

"You have done well, Misi Matt. Accept my thanks. And the thanks of my people."

Matt looked down. Sitting on the palm of his hand was a crusty brown shell.

"Uh, thanks," Matt said. Then he flipped it over and gasped. Underneath the dull, ugly outer layer, the shell was a brilliant, shimmering turquoise blue.

"It's the same color as the ocean and the sky in Samoa," Emily breathed.

Magale smiled. "Yes," he said. "And let it be a reminder to you that, very often, things are not what they seem. A stubborn high chieftain may yet have the humility to admit a mistake. And reckless young boys may indeed have true and honest hearts."

Matt squeezed the shell tight, then slipped it into the pocket of his swim trunks. Magale turned to the colonel.

"We are ready to go with you," he announced.

With his head held high, Magale began walking across the clearing toward the road that led to Pago Pago. The other chieftains followed him. The colonel called for his men to fall in. The soldiers lined up. After waiting for a respectful distance to form between them and the chieftains, the colonel ordered his men forward, and they began their slow return march.

Chapter 12

Misi Tomas, Matt, and Emily were left standing alone outside the meeting-house. Villagers lined the road on both sides and bowed as their high chieftain and other chieftains passed by.

"What will happen to Magale?" Emily asked.

"He will have to go before the governor and explain his actions," Misi Tomas said. "He'll be punished for plotting an uprising. But if the colonel tells the governor about Magale's willingness to call off his warriors, his punishment should not be too severe."

"I don't get it," Matt said. "The soldiers are taking the chieftains to the governor—and they may even go to jail—but look at the people. They're happy!"

Misi Tomas smiled. "The villagers realize that there's a lot to be happy about. Magale is leaving by choice, with dignity and honor. The American soldiers are treating him with the respect his age and position demands. And you've helped prevent a terrible crisis in the Samoan islands. The village is safe. The school is safe. These are things to celebrate."

At his words, an unbelievable combination of wailing, honking, squeaking, and banging filled the air.

"Aha!" cried Misi Tomas delightedly. "The students at the school have heard of your success. Here comes the school band."

"You have a school band?" Matt's eyes shone.

"Of course," Misi Tomas said. "And it's a pretty good one too."

Emily looked at Misi Tomas, watching for any sign that he was joking—but found none. The noise became louder and louder until a short, blond-haired man appeared through the trees. Under one arm he held a shiny saxophone. The other arm was madly waving a stick back and forth in a regular beat. Right behind him came two young boys, enthusiastically banging on drums. They were followed by about a dozen boys of different sizes and ages, all blowing or banging on some kind of instrument.

"Aren't they great?" Misi Tomas said.

"Awesome," Matt said.

"Uh, yeah," Emily said, wondering if anyone would notice if she stuck her fingers in her ears.

Misi Sami spotted Misi Tomas and led the band over to the small group. He waved his arm in a big circle, and with only a few straggler notes, the band fell silent.

"Hi, Misi Tomas," Misi Sami greeted his companion. "The students are celebrating, and I brought Fiti's saxophone so he can join us."

"Great idea," Misi Tomas said. "But I'm afraid Fiti's not up to playing right now. He's still resting at Mama Fiu'u's hut with a head injury."

Misi Sami's expression fell.

"I could play his saxophone instead," Matt volunteered.

"You play the sax?"

"Yeah."

Emily rolled her eyes as Matt accepted

the instrument. The noise was about to get worse.

"And you, Misi Emi? Do you play an instrument?"

Emily shook her head.

"Can you lead music?"

"Not really," she said.

"But you can feel a beat?" Misi Sami pressed.

"Well, yes, I guess so."

"Wonderful." Misi Sami handed over his stick. "Wave the baton in the air, and the boys will begin. Just keep the rhythm steady. They'll follow right along."

"But what are they playing?" Emily asked, panic in her voice.

Misi Sami shrugged. "They've learned many of the hymns. You can choose."

"How about something from *Harry Potter*," Matt suggested.

Misi Sami looked puzzled. "Harry Potter? I haven't heard of him. Is he a new composer?"

Emily shoved her elbow into Matt's side.

"Er, no," Matt said, moving out of Emily's elbow range. "Let's do one of the hymns. You choose one, Misi Tomas."

"How about 'Let Us All Press On'?" the missionary suggested.

Emily smiled with relief. "I know that one," she said.

"All right boys! Misi Emi is your conductor. Follow her lead. We're going to march down to the village and back. Misi Tomas and I will go ahead to check on Fiti."

Nervously, Emily raised the baton in the air. Immediately the noise began. She waved it up and down. The noise grew. And so, not knowing what else to do, she started marching, singing the hymn, and waving her baton up and down as she went. The boys followed.

Across the clearing they went—then down the dirt road and into the center of the village. With the procession of chieftains and soldiers gone, the villagers had returned home. But as the band drew closer, they left what they were doing and gathered around to watch. They cheered and waved as the band passed. Some of the little children ran after them. The joy and enthusiasm that the band members had for their playing was passed to everyone in the village. At last they reached Mama Fiu'u's hut. Standing outside, supported on either side by Misi Tomas and Misi Sami, was Fiti. The nonu leaves were off his face, and the swelling already seemed better.

"Hey, Fiti!" Matt yelled. "Come join us!"

Emily kept the rhythm going with her baton and marched in place. Behind her, the boys marched in place too. With Misi Sami's and Misi Tomas's help, Fiti shuffled forward. He gave Emily a lopsided grin, then took his place beside Matt. Matt offered him the saxophone, but Fiti shook his head.

"You play. I will just try and keep up with the marching."

Emily led the band around the large fire pit and back up the road. She could smell dinner cooking beneath the banana leaves. The band started yet another verse of "Let Us All Press On," and above the random squeaks and honks, Emily could actually make out the tune. She kept the beat going strong all the way to the clearing.

The meetinghouse stood before them, and around one of the doors on the upper level, a strange blue light was glowing. Emily's arm faltered. Behind her, one of the drummers missed the beat. She waved the baton in a big circle, and the musicians blew and banged their final notes.

"You were awesome!" Emily shouted. And this time she really meant it.

The boys smiled. Most of them sat down and rested their instruments across their knees. A few crowded around Fiti and the missionaries, inspecting Fiti's purple eye and showering him with questions. Emily moved closer to her brother.

"Matt," she whispered, "check out the door at the end of the balcony."

Matt glanced over at the meeting-house.

"It's time to go," he said.

With Fiti's saxophone in his hands, Matt approached his Samoan friend.

"Here, Fiti," he said over the boys' excited chatter. He handed over the instrument. "Misi Emi and I have to leave. But thanks . . . thanks for everything."

Fiti accepted the saxophone with a puzzled expression. "Why are you leaving now?"

"I think we've done what we were sent here to do," Emily said.

Misi Tomas overheard her. "And done it very well," he added, stepping forward to shake Matt's hand and then Emily's. "Thank you—on behalf of the Samoan people and the American missionaries."

"And me," Fiti added. "I will not forget you, my friends."

"We'll never forget you either," Matt said.

Fiti smiled.

Matt and Emily smiled back. Then, with a final wave to the band, they took off running. When they reached the meetinghouse, they took the creaking stairs two steps at a time and hurried along the balcony. The bluish light was still streaming out around the door. Matt reached for the doorknob, then hesitated. So much had happened since they'd first seen the magnificent mountains and wild jungle of Samoa—and so much had changed. This time there were no raised voices coming from the council room beneath them and no painted warriors emerging from the trees around the clearing. Instead, the school band had started playing again.

"They'd be all over *Star Wars* music!" he said.

"Yeah, well I'm glad you didn't suggest that along with *Harry Potter*."

Matt looked a little sheepish, "I just forgot . . ." He stopped. "Do you recognize what they're playing now?" he asked.

Emily listened more carefully. "Yes," she said quietly. "'God Be with You Till We Meet Again.'"

With a pleased smile, Matt nodded. "You've come a long way in music appreciation, Sis."

He turned the doorknob and stepped inside. Emily followed and closed the door behind them. The envelope was glowing on the battered wooden desk—exactly where they'd left it. Emily picked it up. Matt took off his name tag and handed it to his sister. Emily unpinned hers and dropped them both into the envelope. As she slid the envelope onto the desk, the blue light in the room swirled, and they heard a low-pitched humming sound. Then silence.

The children waited, staring at the shed door. There was no sound from the other side, and the bluish light was fading fast.

"What do you think?" Emily asked.

Matt moved closer to the door and put his ear to the wood. "Hmm," he said. "There's a delicious woodworm in the second panel, but no sound of a school band outside."

"Very funny!"

Matt twisted the doorknob, held it, then gently pulled. When a crack of light appeared, he stopped. He put his eye to the gap and peeked out.

"We're back," he said.

Chapter 13

Very carefully, Matt opened the shed door a little wider and looked both ways.

"I don't see anyone."

"Okay, let's go." Emily moved up behind him and gave him a gentle push. "Hurry!"

They stepped outside, and Emily pulled the door shut behind them. Within seconds, they were standing beneath the wall that separated the MTC from their backyard. Quickly, Emily bent over and cupped her hands together. Matt placed his foot in Emily's waiting hands, and she hiked him upward. As soon as he was safely on top of the wall, Matt reached down to help his sister, and she scrambled up beside him.

"Ouch! That hurt," she said, pausing long enough to check her scraped knee. "Next time, were using a ladder or rope."

"Do you think there'll be a next time?" Matt asked.

Emily looked down at the shed.

Everything looked so normal—no bluish light, no humming—nothing that would set it apart from any other shed anywhere.

"When we're back home, it's hard to believe anything unusual could ever happen," she said.

Matt put his hand in his pocket and withdrew the shell Magale had given him. He turned it over in his hand, studying the plain, crusty brown outside and the shining, shimmering blue inside.

"Yeah," he agreed. "But it *has* happened—twice." He looked at Emily. "And I think it'll happen again."

"I wonder where it'll be next time?" Emily said.

Matt started climbing down the ash tree. "I don't know, but I'm going to put this shell in the box where I put the German mark. Then I think I'll go practice the saxophone some more."

"But what about swimming? Mom might be back by now."

"Exactly!" Matt called over his shoulder. "I'll distract her with my impressive playing so you can change into your other swimsuit."

Emily looked down at her swimsuit and wrinkled her nose. Matt was right.

Her clothes still smelled, and the salty sea water had only slightly faded the stains she'd picked up in the Cave of the Flying Foxes. She started down the tree as fast as she could.

"Cover me for ten minutes," she called.

"I'll give you one verse of 'Let Us All Press On,'" Matt yelled back with a grin. Then he disappeared inside the house.

Emily started to run.

Author's Note

Matt and Emily's adventure in Samoa is fictitious, but the experience of Misi Tomas is based on the true story of Elder W. Karl Brewer. When Elder Brewer first arrived on the island of Tutuila, American Samoa, in 1921, his mission president, John Q. Adams, gave him a list of duties that included the following:

Teach in one of our eighteen schools.
Put in time (short) on a Church plantation.
Eat, almost exclusively, the native food.

Learn the native language. Use it exclusively.
Study, pray, and work, steadily, of course.
Tramp about the steep volcanic rocky trails.
Ride in small boats and face seasickness.
Sleep on a mat on a stone floor (no pillow).
Sleep imprisoned in a mosquito-proof net.
Often wash own clothes (no ironing).

Elder Brewer, who was renamed Misi Paine by the Samoan people, did indeed experience these things during his mission. For several months, he taught at the Church school in Mapusaga, where, among other things, the missionaries developed a fine band and orchestra program. He also organized the clearing of the Church-owned coconut plantation, which created a new source of income for the people of Mapusaga, along with an unprecedented increase in tithing payments.

Elder Brewer learned to enjoy many Samoan foods including steamed pig, fish, taro, breadfruit, and palusami. He and the other missionaries usually ate with the villagers at the type of communal dinner described in the book. There was one Samoan delicacy, however, that Elder Brewer could never bring himself to try—the wood-worm.

One day, while he was serving in Mapusaga, Elder Brewer happened to see a group of warriors running through the village. This was such an unusual sight that Elder Brewer hurried to the home of one of the village leaders to find out what was happening. The man told Elder Brewer that Magale, the high chieftain of the island, had placed a formal petition with the governor, and that when his request was denied, he had become very angry and had decided to go to war against the American government.

Elder Brewer immediately realized the gravity of the situation. He broke with Samoan protocol and interrupted the chieftain's council meeting, where he appealed to Magale to reconsider his actions. When Elder Brewer explained the probable outcome of war with the American government, Magale agreed to call off the ambush he had planned. He sent runners to the warriors who were lying in wait for the American soldiers. The runners were able to pass on the message in time to avert disaster.

When the soldiers arrived in Mapusaga, the officer in charge entered the meetinghouse, bowed to Magale, then bowed to the other chieftains. Magale rose majestically and said, "We are ready to go with you." He left the council room and started down the road to Pago Pago, followed by the other chieftains and, at a respectful distance, the soldiers.

Anxious to request leniency for Magale and the other chieftains, Elder Brewer arranged a meeting with the governor. He explained that the Samoans did not realize how serious a step they were taking in deciding to fight the soldiers. To them it was simply a matter of making a strong stand for their rights—a stand they might take with any other village or chieftain. The governor thanked Elder Brewer for taking such an interest in the Samoan chieftains and for helping to avoid any bloodshed.

The chieftains were sent to trial. Magale and two other chieftains were found guilty of planning the uprising. To fulfill the law, they were sent to prison while the others were free to return to their villages.

Elder Brewer went to visit Magale in prison several times, but the high chieftain did not have to stay there for long. A chieftain is expected to be courteous and gracious to everyone, and Magale was an honorable chieftain. His sentence was quickly reduced for model behavior.

Although Mama Fiu'u is fictitious, the Samoan saying that she quoted is not. The nonu plant is commonly used for medicinal purposes among the Samoan people. Throughout the Pacific Islands, the nonu fruit, leaves, bark, and flowers are used to cure everything from infections to stomach aches, diabetes to tonsillitis, toothaches to high blood pressure. In Samoa, in particular, the nonu leaves are prescribed for rheumatism and swelling.

Sources

Brewer, Karl W. *Armed with the Spirit: Missionary Experiences in Samoa*. Provo, UT: Brigham Young University Press, 1975.

Hart, John W., Glen Wright, and Allan D. Patterson. *History of Samoa*. Pesega, Apia, Western Samoa: Church Schools of Western Samoa, The Church of Jesus Christ of Latter-day Saints, 1972.

http://www.bbc.co.uk/nature/reallywild/amazing/flying_fox.shtml

http://www.naturia.per.sg/buloh/plants/morinda.htm

http://www.ntbg.org/plants/plantresource_new3.php?rid=172&focus=8

About the Author

Siân Ann Bessey was born in Cambridge, England, but grew up on the island of Anglesey off the north coast of Wales. At the age of ten, she joined the Church along with her entire family. Siân left Wales to attend Brigham Young University and graduated with a bachelor's degree in communications.

Siân and her husband, Kent, are the parents of five children. They live in Rexburg, Idaho, and enjoy visiting new places and experiencing different cultures. Siân loves to cook and is constantly trying new recipes. Although she invariably places last when playing games with her family—even when she's up against her six-year-old—she's always invited back to play because she bakes the treats.

In addition to her novels (*Forgotten Notes, Cover of Darkness,* and *Deception*) and her children's books (*A Family Is Forever* and *A Teddy Bear, Blankie, and a Prayer*), Siân has written several articles that have appeared in the *New Era, Ensign,* and *Liahona* magazines. Siân is the Welsh form of Jane, and is pronounced "Shawn."

If you would like to be updated on Siân's newest releases or correspond with her, please send an e-mail to info@covenant-lds.com. You may also write to her in care of Covenant Communications, P.O. Box 416, American Fork, UT 84003-0416.